Touch
Of
Fate

Kate Allenton

Copyright © 2012 Kate Allenton

All rights reserved.

ISBN: 098536842X
ISBN-13: 978-0-9853684-2-5

Touch of Fate

Published by Coastal Escape Publishing

Touch of Fate

DEDICATION

This is dedicated to my best friend Julie,

who's strength and determination inspire me.

To her son, Anthony, who was my inspiration of how a loving and protective son would act toward his mother.

To my mother, who molded me into the woman I've become.

And

To all of the single mothers and fathers, who struggle everyday

raising children by themselves.

May you find your happily ever after.

ACKNOWLEDGMENTS

I want to thank, DRW for pushing me
to perform the impossible.

I want to thank, Brian for listening to
all of my ranting and raving about
my crazy characters.

And all my readers, who've sent me
emails requesting more.

You keep me motivated to continue
on this journey.

Kate Allenton

CHAPTER 1

Out of all the gifts she and her siblings had, Abby Bennett got the gift of psychometry. Her family assumed her ability to read objects with just one touch would make her excel in her career as a forensic investigator, but they were wrong. She'd vowed eighteen years before never to use her so-called gift of heightened senses again. Not after the havoc it had already created in her life. No, there would never be any hocus-pocus in her forensic reports, only the hardcore throw-in-your face facts to put the criminals away.

Abby strolled down the long corridor of the investigation unit toward her office. She was early today. Most of her co-workers hadn't made it in yet, and those from the midnight shift were just packing up to head home.

"The blood splatter was everywhere. You would have loved this one,' Matt Thompson said walking up beside her with a gleam in his hazel eyes.

Matt loved this job as much as she did, and he knew just what to say to grab her attention. There were never any poetic ramblings or promises of a future from the male walking beside her. Only promises of a new criminal to outsmart and another case to help solve. She loved her job, just as much as she hated the murderers who gave her a reason to come into work every day. As long as there were criminals on the street, there were a lot more sleepless nights in her and her co-workers' futures.

Abby strode into her office and put away her things. She turned and smiled at Matt. "I hope you remembered to take the pictures this time."

Matt crossed his arms over his chest and sighed. That was a rookie mistake he had made, not easily forgotten. Heck, they all made them when first starting out; his was just more recent than most, making him an easy target.

I should seriously try to be nice, but who am I kidding? If the officers in her department didn't pick on someone, that meant they didn't like you. It had only taken her a week to figure that one out, well, that and having a big brother on the force. She would hate to see how they treated the women they were dating. Would they pull them by the ponytail and thump their chests? *Men.*

Abby couldn't hide the tilt of her lips when Matt plopped down in the leather chair across from her desk with his shoulder slumped. He looked like he'd just lost his puppy. She knew his wounded look wouldn't last long; a total a ruse for her benefit. Maybe he hoped she would offer to console him and take back her teasing words. There were several dispatchers and female officers she could call who would jump at the chance to be the center of his attention.

Seconds ticked by as Abby stood there with her arms crossed over her chest, silently wondering when he would grow up. At the age of thirty, Matt was six years her junior and still had a thing or two to learn about women in general, and even more than a few to learn about her. "Well, did you take pictures or not?"

Matt slowly looked up. The twinkle in his eyes confirmed her suspicion. Yep, he was trying to play the sympathy card. Abby sighed and sat down, placing her folded arms on the desk.

He smiled. "Of course I did. What do you think? I'm a rookie?"

Matt had moved into town about six months before and hadn't been in her department long. Regardless of his short time here, they shared the thrill of the job. Her gaze went up to his face as his traveled down to her chest. His pretty-boy looks of high cheekbones and dimples might work on the other women in the office, but not her. Although, she would have to be dead not to enjoy the six-pack abs she'd seen while working out with him in the department's gym. He was everything a woman could want. Just not her. She couldn't figure out why she wasn't drooling like the rest of the women in the office. No tingly sensations seized her body; only a friendship had started to bloom. *What the hell is wrong with me?*

Matt's grin got bigger. Just what she needed, another co-worker who thought he was a god. Abby raised her brows and leaned across the desk, holding out her hand. "Well, what are you waiting for? Let me see."

He placed the file in her hands, and she ignored the slight graze of his fingers against hers. Abby flipped open the file, getting down to business when she leaned over the pictures in front of her, analyzing every single detail of the graphic blood splatter displayed in crimson color.

A knock on her doorframe interrupted her train of thought.

"Hey, Abby, we've got a case. Grab your gear," her captain said as he tapped the doorframe once more and vanished down the hall.

A shot of adrenaline pulsed through her veins, something to keep her occupied from what awaited her tomorrow. Her heart raced as she handed the file back over to Matt. Smiling, she stood. "Gotta go catch me some bad guys."

Matt exited her office with her and walked in step with her short strides down the hall. Her thoughts were solely on what she might find waiting for her. As much as she loved what she did, she sometimes dreaded finding out the facts. Most of these victims had families and loved ones that would miss them, and that sobering thought usually kept her grounded.

Abby and her siblings had grown up in the little lake town of Southall, North Carolina. She could remember a time, back when they were younger, when unlocked doors and playing outside after dark were the norm. Those times were now a thing of the past. The town had grown over the years, filled now with people she didn't know, and with growth came criminals and a new wave of crime keeping her entire department busy.

"Abby, I was thinking."

She stopped in her tracks and closed her eyes briefly, letting out a breath. She opened her eyes in time to see his hazel eyes sparkle as they ran the length of her body, drinking her up, eventually landing on her face. His smile held hints of promises she was sure he could deliver.

Here it comes, the same question he'd been asking for the last two weeks. She let out another long sigh. "Yeah?"

He cleared his throat. "How about you let me take you on a date?" His cheeks tinted with a hint of red. Abby didn't know what she would do with a man so full of confidence one minute and filled with embarrassment the next. His lack of confidence was his only downfall. It was the reason Abby ultimately kept him in friend status, no matter what other assets he had to offer.

"Matt, you know I like you, and we get along great. I don't doubt for a minute that we'd click in all other areas..." She cleared her throat. "Outside of work, but you know I don't date coworkers." Abby gave him a smile and kept walking, hoping he wouldn't press the issue. She had fallen for his type before, good looking with a killer smile. *Been there done that.* A similar perfect package gifted her with the task of raising a child by herself. She wasn't naive enough to go there again, at least not without condoms.

Matt hollered after her. "Aw, Abby, don't make me quit my job. I like it here."

Abby spun on her heels, turning back to him. Matt winked then walked away, leaving her to stare at his retreating body.

****

Abby arrived on the scene in the old part of town. Crumbling apartment buildings surrounded her as she took in all of the emergency vehicles, cruisers, and the coroner van parked nearby. Onlookers stood in the courtyard, corralled by the crime scene tape trying to get a peek, and she silently wondered if the killer was brave enough to be among them. Keeping the crime scene contained was going to be a nightmare; thankfully, that wasn't her job. She ducked underneath the crime scene tape and entered the old apartment.

The putrid smell of the blood was the first to assault her senses. She covered her mouth with her hand, hoping not to gag from the smell. That would be a rookie mistake she hadn't made in years. *Will I ever get used to this?* She swallowed the lump in her throat and passed through the foyer to the living room. She could imagine how the place looked without the broken furniture littering the floor. It wasn't the best of places, but it wasn't the worst she'd seen. Trinkets and books covered the shelves. The victim cared about her dwelling and it showed.

Henry, the old grey-haired coroner, was on bended knee next to the body, careful not to touch, observing what he could without disturbing the evidence. His years of experience were invaluable in their line of work, and Henry had seen a lot in those years. There were few people Abby trusted, but Henry was unquestionably one of them.

"What've we got?" Abby asked, stepping over the splintered wood pieces from the broken furniture scattered around the room. *She put up a fight.*

"Female, Caucasian, late forties, early fifties multiple lacerations to her upper torso, bruising on her wrist, and a red mark around her neck."

"Hand prints? Rope? What do you think?" Abby knelt down to get a better view for herself.

"If I had to guess, rope around the wrists, but I'm not sure about the neck. Not fingerprints, maybe marks from a necklace. The placement of her stab wounds through her major arteries and heart is probably what killed her, but I won't know for sure until I get her back to the morgue." Henry was rubbing his grey beard, tilting his head from side to side, as if he were afraid to miss something from a different angle.

"Let me grab my camera, and I'll get started." She sat her trusty bag full of equipment down on the floor nearby, slipped on her latex gloves, and pulled out her camera and the numbered markers. She'd processed so many crime scenes; the tasks came second nature to her. Even though the scene was never identical, her methods were.

"Do you know if this place has any type of security system?"

Henry never paused in his assessment, not even to answer her. His gaze trained on the lifeless female body. "Jefferson is headed to the manager's office, and several other officers left to question witnesses and canvas the area." He shrugged. "Maybe we'll get lucky."

Somehow she doubted it, but it wouldn't be from the lack of trying. Jefferson had been with the department as long as her brother, Mike, had and was just as good. The motionless body lay facing the sliding glass door, as if she had attempted to make a run for it after being stabbed. The wall that adjoined the kitchen had most of the blood splattered in an arc. Her queasy stomach rolled from the sight. The unease sent a slight shiver down her spine.

"Let's catch this creep," she mumbled. Abby remembered each victim and every crime, locking it in her brain should she ever have the need to recall the information again. She would catalogue this one too. *This bastard is going down.* No one deserved this type of death. A thought occurred and Abby walked back to the door checking the locks and the surrounding frames. She proceeded back into the apartment and checked the windows. No forced entry. *She opened the door.* Possibly someone she knew and if not, someone she didn't feel threatened by. Abby couldn't fathom the pain the victim had felt or the darkness of the killer who had done the deed. She shook off the slight chill to refocus on her task.

Crimson stains now covered the pale walls and told a scene all of its own. Each piece of evidence was like trying to solve a puzzle. If you missed just one, you would only have fragments of the picture.

The tail end of the blood spray had dried dripping to the right. "The killer is left-handed or at least ambidextrous." *So much blood.* She wondered if maybe some of the killer's might be mixed in. Abby hoped the victim might have gotten in a hit or two against her murderer while struggling for her life. She numbered the evidence and continued to snap photos and swab some blood from the walls and around the body. Henry informed her, from his observation the visual lacerations were deep and had been made from an angle. Her perp was taller then the victim's roughly five-foot-six frame. This was not going to be an easy case. No crying boyfriend stood nearby, no blood-covered knife lay around waiting to be dust for finger prints, and damn it there was no confession.

Abby snapped more pictures as she made her way around the room then hit play on the blinking answering machine. A high-pitched, panicked voice shrilled through the speakers, a mother's urgent request to call her, a message that would sadly go unanswered. She pulled the tape and bagged it to listen to the rest at the lab. With any luck, maybe their perp had left a message and the phone records would lead them in the right direction.

Processing the scene took a few hours. She collected tiny fibers along with skin from underneath the victim's nails for further analysis. She didn't need the cigarettes in the ashtray to tell her the victim was a smoker. Her house reeked from it. Her clothes, even the walls, held a dull yellow tint. She bagged the discarded butts. The contents of her purse lying spilled on the floor would hold clues to her identity. Her fingers skimmed over the driver's license, turning it over in her fingers as a vision hit, pulling her mind to an unknown place. Their victim, dressed as a waitress, was smiling down at a table full of men. Her low cut blouse was missing a button. Abby's attention was drawn by the light shining through the window as it sparkled off a trinket lying between the swells of her breasts. *A locket*. She dismissed the scene as she always did. What she wanted were the facts she could prove.

Henry must have seen the faraway look on her face and decided it was time to bring her back to reality. He was one of the few besides her family that knew her secret, touching objects in her job was essential. She figured it wouldn't take him too long to figure out something was off when she was zoned out. "Abby, isn't your sister's wedding tomorrow?"

Abby sighed, remembering her sister Emma's own escape from a deranged lunatic not too long before. She was happy Emma had come out of the attack unscathed and elated that she'd found love in the process. Her lips curved at the thought. "Yep, tomorrow at three o'clock."

"Why are you here today?"

"I only planned to come in for a few hours." She shrugged. "I'm just going to collect evidence. I won't have time to start processing it before Emma's next crisis hits. If I don't keep busy, Emma will drive me crazy." Abby smiled for the first time since arriving.

Her sister Emma might be a nutcase like her, but she had been fortunate to find true love. Even the crazy ghost, Momma Mae, that up until recently only Emma could see, had shown herself to Abby's soon-to-be brother-in-law. Jake had been a godsend in saving Emma from her deranged ex-boyfriend and ultimately winning her heart. Abby shivered at the memory of Emma's abduction. They all had a lot to be thankful for and to celebrate.

Abby took the last of her pictures in the living room and rounded the corner to the small bedroom. *What the hell?* A unique symbol had been drawn in blood on the wall above the bed. A five-pointed star-shaped pentagram surrounded the initials RD. It couldn't be that easy. The RD didn't stand for their victim. The name on the driver's license was Sara Johnson.

"What the hell does the RD stand for?" she mumbled, and snapped a few more digital pictures. *What is this sick bastard trying to tell us?*

"Not sure, but Jones and I will finish up here."

"Thanks, Henry. I'm heading back to the lab, and I'll call you after the wedding." She discarded her gloves and bagged them too. Her heart was heavy as she exited the apartment with her camera still attached around her neck and stopped. The curious onlookers stood in the courtyard, enthralled by the unknown. She snapped their pictures, several people in the group at one time, before putting her lens cover back on. *If you're here, I've got you.* Abby only hoped the killer was stupid or deranged enough to have stuck around to be included in the shot.

****

He stood in the shadows watching the police mill around. His lips tilted up in a smile as he turned to leave, only stopping when a little brunette leaving the slut's apartment caught his eye. She aimed her camera toward him and others standing around. They wouldn't find anything he hadn't wanted them to. They never did. He grinned and turned his head and body to avoid the shot. He had some planning to do before his real target showed up and he knew it wouldn't be long.

****

Back at the lab, she logged and stored the evidence to be processed. The pentagram drawing stayed heavy on her mind. She just couldn't shake the fact it was important and vital to the investigation. With a digital copy of the mysterious pentagram in hand, she grabbed her things and left the lab. Her sister's frantic wedding call about her dress had interrupted her, so she was heading home early. Something wasn't right; she shivered. She'd missed something and knew it. She balled her hands, partially crinkling the pictures grasped between her fingers. She headed down the hall toward the one man she knew could help. Ted was the smartest man she knew. He was bound to be able to make some sense out of this mess. Ted had been instrumental in helping track down her kidnapped sister and was one of the reasons Emma was still alive.

Abby found him in the hall with a can of soda in his hands. "Hey, Ted, can you do me a favor?"

"Two in one year, miracles never cease."

He was like an extended part of her family. The snide comments were expected. "Smart ass, can you run this picture through your database and see if you hit on anything? I have a feeling this isn't the first time this perp has killed."

He took the picture and squinted his eyes as he did his visual perusal. "Five star pentagram, Ancient Greece, Wiccans, Star of David, magical, five wounds of Jesus, a symbol of faith to many Christians, a way to summon the elements for others. Many symbols for good and evil, depending on the beliefs of the person who drew it." He looked up and pulled in a breath.

"I'm more interested in the letters in the middle."

He turned retreating back down the hall to his office, when he called over his shoulder. "I'm on it."

He lived to solve the riddles the rest of them couldn't figure out. If anyone could figure it out, it would be Ted.

"Thanks" she said, throwing her purse over her shoulder and heading

Kate Allenton

toward the parking garage to deal with Emma and her wedding issues.

CHAPTER 2

John's graduation a few months before had left her feeling older than thirty-six. Her son was all grown up now, a man by society's standards; however, he would always be her baby. Single and alone were the cards she'd been dealt, but she had her fallbacks. Abby loved the thrill of hunting the bad guys and had her family and friends to keep her company. Still, she felt lonely down into her core and had a void she couldn't figure out how to fill.

Abby glanced in the mirror one last time. Her tired, bloodshot eyes

Kate Allenton

stared back at her. There wasn't enough makeup in the world to hide the puffiness that had made a home under her eyes. The long hours and stress from work showed on her face. Many nights she'd brought her work home with her unable to sleep until the victims rested in peace. It was a wonder John hadn't grown up mentally scarred by some of the pictures she had left on the dining room table during his life.

She liked helping people, making them feel safe by taking the bad guys off the street. Her hopes and dreams had taken on an entirely new shape after her dad's murder the need for justice propelled her into a profession she hadn't ever thought of entering. Forensic investigation was now her passion. She absorbed everything, and she never got enough to satisfy her curiosity. The truth fueled her. She thrived on the in-your-face facts she could prove, refusing to use the nonsense visions her gift gave her. The damn thing had let her down enough when she had needed it most.

Abby grabbed the old brush on the dresser and clutched it close to her heart, closing her eyes. Images of her mother's face appeared behind her eyelids. Abby watched her mother's stunning blue eyes sparkle as she looked through the mirror at a ten year Emma, as she ran a brush through her long brown locks. Emma looked just about ten years old and was missing a tooth as she smiled back. That was why Abby had kept the old brush. It was the only link she still had to her mom to bring back memories long forgotten.

Abby opened her eyes back to reality. Her son, John, was propped up against her doorframe, offering her a sad smile and a nod of understanding. John's beautiful blue eyes and deep-set dimples instantly triggered memories of the man she had once loved. Abby pushed those thoughts back to the recess of her mind now focusing on the man that stood in front of her. Her son was the one man that had been a constant in her life unlike the man that had helped create him.

"Mom, we're going to be late."

"No, we're not. Your Aunt Emma is never on time, so we'll still be early." Abby's lips tilted up.

"You're forgetting that Jake is always on time. She wouldn't dare be late to her own wedding." John rolled his eyes, a gesture she had seen all through out his life.

Her brother-in-law might be new to the family, but he wasn't stupid. He'd realized how special her sister was from the first time they'd met, and Emma had fallen hard for him. It was only fitting they get married and live happily ever after. *Someone in the family should.* Abby and her siblings owed Jake everything for saving Emma's life from the psychopaths set on revenge. Abby sighed, coming out of her thoughts. She straightened her mauve bridesmaid dress and walked toward her son.

John pushed off from the doorframe, standing up straight. "I'm riding with the silent giant, but Butch is in the living room waiting to take you. He knows you need to be there early."

"Briggs would kill you if he knew you called him that." She chuckled.

"Nah, Aunt Claire said I could." Her soon-to-be brother-in-law, Jake, had assigned Briggs to her older sister, Claire, during the whole Emma fiasco while their brother, Mike, helped Abby track down the killer.

Jake's coworkers were like extended family now. Their secrets had been exposed during the kidnapping. It was refreshing having friends you could be yourself with, flaws and all that didn't judge.

"Okay, baby, I'll see you there."

John pulled her into a warm embrace and placed a kiss on her forehead. "You look beautiful, Mom."

A tear trickled down her cheek. She had been extremely lucky her son had grown into a good man, during his early teens it had been touch and go until he grew out of his defiant stage. "Thank you, baby."

Butch called from the living room, "Let's go, princess. Jake will have my head if you're late."

Abby applied the last coat of pink-tinted gloss to her lips and sauntered out of her room, giving a little twirl to show off the dress she had helped pick out.

Butch was silent, and his eyes twinkled with his mouth parted. She enjoyed the brief shock on his face. The man that had once scared her stood like a vision of a Greek god in her living room. His black tuxedo stretched over taut muscles that Abby had seen up close and personal only months before when Butch had been tasked with babysitting and keeping her safe. Of all of Jake's friends, Butch was the one she felt closest to and felt a connection with.

"Well, aren't you handsome?" Abby said. Butch picked up her hand and placed a gentle kiss on top of her gloves.

"You look beautiful, Abby. Remind me to thank Emma later for making you wear that dress." He smiled. His eyes traveled the length of her body and back up, stopping at her cleavage. She chuckled.

His eyebrows danced up and down as his grin grew. He leaned over her and whispered in her ear while looking down her dress, "Show me where you're hiding your weapon."

She reached down and adjusted the slit in her dress, revealing her creamy thigh-high stockings held up by a black garter belt and the holster she had attached to the top of her thigh.

"Hot damn."

"You've seen enough. If we're late, I'm telling Emma it was your fault." Abby smiled and grabbed her clutch, stuffing her phone inside. She hadn't had a chance to close her purse before her cell started to ring. She checked the caller ID and hit speaker. "Speak to me."

"Hey, doll face, you must have been right about that picture."

She stopped gathering her things and stared at the phone clutched in her hand.

"What picture, doll face?" Butch asked.

She hushed him and returned her focus on the phone.

"Sorry, that was Butch; you know how nosy he is." She turned and smiled at him. "What did you find out?"

"Nothing." He sounded perplexed. "But it must have been something. The FBI showed up today demanding to talk to the investigators."

"Really? Well, that is interesting. What did the captain tell them?"

"You were headed to a wedding, and that was all I heard."

"Thanks for the heads-up. I guess I'll get the details tomorrow." Abby counted on him to be her eyes and ears.

"Keep me posted if there's anything else I can do for you. I'll be calling in those favors when my mother comes into town." He chuckled.

"You got it, and Ted...thanks again." Abby flipped her phone closed, turned it off, and shoved it in her purse as she sauntered out of the house on the arm of one of her new best friends.

CHAPTER 3

Abby stood oblivious to the crowd behind her with her champagne flute in hand, staring toward the orange and red sun as it lowered beneath the horizon. She smiled. *This is what peace feels like.* Her heart felt full for the first time in years, happy for her sister and the union with the man she loved. The reception was ending, like the old chapters in her sister's life. Emma's happily ever after was just beginning with the promise of

new memories to create and happier
times yet to come. The sound of
clinking glasses and conversations
carried on behind her. Abby ignored
it all, soaking in the serenity that the
moment had to offer. A gentle touch
on her arm pulled her from her
solitude. She inhaled a deep breath
and admired the fleeting sunset once
more before she plastered a smile on
her face and turned to greet the
awaiting wedding guest vying for her
attention.

Recognition hit her like a punch
in the gut. Her smile fell just like the
champagne flute from her hand,
which now lay in broken shards on
the floor. She stepped back
instinctively. A ghost from her past,
the one man she had searched for,
for the last eighteen years, stood a
foot away. The same man that had
altered her life forever. She felt the
blood drain from her face and her
world start to spin as her gaze locked
with his.

"Abby, you're just as beautiful as
I remember." His smile reached his

eyes that glistened under the twinkling lights.

"Ryan," she whispered, unable to do more. The years barely showed; his handsome features remained unchanged. Eyes the color of sapphires stared back at her. The same smile that had stolen her heart so long ago was once again etched across his lips. Her muscles tensed as she tried to push down the lump in her throat. The wall around her heart constricted and faltered for a brief moment. Her brain refused to process what he was doing here, hell, that he was actually here at all.

"I've missed you," he replied as he took a step in her direction.

The crunch of glass beneath his shoes brought her out of her daze. Abby flinched as his hand lifted to touch her. The same hand that had brought her pleasure years ago now brought a cold chill. Her feet froze in place; she was unable to flee. She shook her head in disbelief as she tried to regain her composure. No, she wouldn't let this man get to her, not again.

Kate Allenton

She wasn't the same naive girl from before and hadn't been in a long time, he'd made sure of that. Becoming a mother had changed everything. He didn't even know her anymore, and he'd never known his son. Abby had imagined this moment for the last eighteen years of her life, yet no words slipped past her lips.

This man was a stranger and a liar. Angry tears threatened to fall. She clenched her fists tight, digging her nails into her palms. Her blood boiled at all the lost years she would never get back crying over the one man who had hurt her beyond repair. *Why is he here? How dare he be here!* Abby pulled her arm back and swung her clenched fist, hitting her intended target in the cheek. His head jerked to the side, unprepared for her reaction to his presence.

She let out a breath and rubbed her throbbing hand as pain radiated up her arm. She hadn't dropped him on his ass as she had planned all those years ago, but an instant red mark appeared, satisfying the anger she felt inside.

"Abby, please let me explain." He held his hand out to her in a silent plea.

"Don't you dare fucking touch me. You lost your chance eighteen years ago, Ryan, or whatever the hell your real name is."

She turned, took two steps, and paused, spinning around to face him once more. "Go to hell, Ryan!" she said as she stomped off in search of her sisters. Abby's pooling tears fell as her heart threatened to beat out of her chest. *This isn't happening.*

There was no way in hell she was ever going to forgive that man.

****

Richard Daley stood in the shadows of the prestigious country club watching his prey. Women dressed in their Sunday best congregated in the hall as they drank and discussed the bride's dress, all of them oblivious that he stood within reach ready to claim his intended target. Obscured from view was how he liked it, how he needed it. His

Kate Allenton

pulse quickened. He'd known Ryan would show up at the police station. Hell, he'd left him his signature calling card. He always showed up, but this time was going to be different. *Much different.* Following Ryan to this place hadn't even been a challenge. The pimple-faced teen that threatened his freedom from eighteen years ago had turned into a man. Ryan lingered nearby, striking out with the same little brunette from the slut's house yesterday.

There were no coy whispers to tease him. This conversation was for the world to hear. The brunette stood with her mouth hanging open, and her fists clenched. Then she pressed those luscious pink lips tight in a line, and he knew what she was going to do next, even if Ryan didn't see it coming. She drew her fist back and swung, hitting the only man who had ever witnessed his sins. Ryan Douglas was going to die if the brunette didn't kill him first. He chuckled. *Yes, this feisty little one is the key. I'm going to have fun this time, and in the end, she's going to be mine.*

Ryan Douglas looked like a teenager, his uncertainty written all over his face as the conversation progressed leaving him no prospect of an easy night. He would be leaving this party alone, well, at least without the sexy spitfire on his arm. He had struck out with the beauty but refused to retreat. *Interesting.* Richard pulled back in the shadows to devise a new plan, one that would now include this little brunette in Ryan's death.

CHAPTER 4

Abby stopped at the bar and ordered a drink, when she couldn't find her sister. She threw her head back, emptying the clear liquid from the little glass. She coughed. The shot of tequila burned going down her throat, reminding her, she had survived the encounter and was still alive. Her brother Mike and her new brother-in-law, Jake, slowly approached. Able to read her mood, they held their hands up in surrender; clearly, they had witnessed the exchange, but she doubted Mike recognized the man.

She turned her back on them and ordered a beer. Mike walked up behind her and gently rubbed her arms and got the information he wanted. Mike's gift had never failed him, unlike hers. Mike could touch someone and see the truth in his mind. Like a movie playing in his head. He could even pick up things the mind refused to recall. That little secret helped make him such a talented detective.

"Holy shit. You have got to be kidding me. After all these years, he shows up today, of all days."

"You took the words right out of my mouth," she said, throwing her head back and taking a large swallow of her beer. The alcohol did little to numb her mind or her throbbing hand. Her shoulders slumped as she leaned against the bar. Her head hanging low, she tried to figure out if she'd done the right thing. She lifted her head just in time to see Ryan's approach. Abby didn't have the gift of sight and seeing into the future, but she didn't need it to know what was about to happen. Mike's temper was bound to get the best of him, and Abby refused to let it be over this man. No, this man was her problem. She grabbed Mike's arm, bringing his attention to focus back to her.

"He's not worth it." She drained the beer then set the empty bottle on the bar. "Jake, tell Emma I'm sorry I had to leave and I'll call her tomorrow. Please try your best to keep Mike in line."

She twisted her hands as she scanned the dance floor and mumbled, "I...I need to find Butch. That's what I need to do." Abby left them standing there to look for her one and only protector, who happened to be her ride for the night.

A tear slid down her cheek in front of a room full of family and friends, and that did nothing but piss her off. The sight of him had opened wounds that had finally started to heal.

Her family would handle him. She just needed to escape and get her head on straight. Abby thought she'd been preparing herself all her life to seek Ryan again, but she'd been wrong. The encounter left her ready to collapse on her feet, physically and emotionally drained from the wedding and the unwanted guest. Her family meant the world to her and was the only thing she had left. They had been her rock when she was a young woman with a toddler in tow, trying to make a future for them both. They had always been her cheering section, pushing her to be a better person. Since Butch had begun babysitting her, she'd grown close to him too, and he was who she needed now.

Abby made a beeline for Butch, her one and only protector, assigned to keep her safe when Emma had been in danger. The man had grown on her. His outrageous comments and constant flirting always seemed to lift her spirits even in the dire of circumstances. He made her laugh, which was exactly what she needed right now. Abby stood off to the side of the dance floor. Her gaze locked with Butch's when another tear slid down her cheek.

He excused himself from the blonde draped around his neck, nestled his arm around Abby's shoulder, and pulled her close to his side, placing a kiss on the top of her head. Abby leaned into him, taking the support he offered as he led her from the room. He didn't ask questions, just escorted her out, almost as if he had read her mind and knew what her heart required at that precise moment. Abby needed the comfort only a close friend could provide, one that wouldn't press her with questions or require a conversation and would let her sulk for the time in the comfort of her own mind.

***

Mike watched Ryan march up to him and Jake.

"Where did she go and who the hell was that she left with?" Ryan demanded, a hint of annoyance in his tone.

A muscle twitched in Mike's jaw. Every muscle in his body strung

Kate Allenton

tight, he was ready to kill the bastard who had hurt his baby sister all those years ago.

"None of your fucking business," Mike spouted.

Jake placed a restraining hand on Mike's shoulder. "Don't ruin this for Emma. I'll handle it."

"Actually, I was told to find her brother, Mike if I couldn't find Abby, and if I had to guess, then I'm betting that would be you." the wedding intruder exclaimed.

"By who?" Mike and Jake barked out in unison.

"Your captain."

"Bullshit," Mike said as he pulled his cell out of his tuxedo pants pocket, punching numbers to figure out what the hell was going on. He shared a look and a silent nod with Jake as he confirmed the situation.

Mike's voice grew louder. He couldn't believe what he was hearing. "Like hell. No, sir, she isn't working with him. Assign someone else. Yes, sir, I know she's the best, but you can't possibly ask her to do this. I'll explain everything in the morning.

No, sir, she isn't going to like this. Yes, sir, I'll tell her." He flipped his phone closed and took a step closer toward Ryan, infringing on his personal space.

"Don't think you can hide behind your badge, asshole. If you mess with her again, I won't be the only one you'll have to worry about."

Ryan cleared his throat and crossed his arms over his chest. "That's between me and Abby, and we'll deal with the past later. I'm here on business tonight, and I need to ask her some questions. Where'd she go?"

"She's off the clock asshole. You're going to have to wait until tomorrow to talk to her." Mike smirked when Ryan left the club without so much as a backwards glance. He called out to Ryan's retreating back, "See you at headquarters." He took a deep breath then muttered, "Bastard."

CHAPTER 5

Abby arrived home with her emotions ranging all over the chart. She curled up on her couch, wrinkling her mauve bridesmaid dress, and let the tears fall free, retreating inward to a safe place Ryan couldn't touch. The vise around her heart clenched, and she was unable to escape the replay of his words through her thoughts, wondering what they meant. She didn't know if minutes or hours had passed as she tried to make sense of

Kate Allenton

how his presence might affect her and John's life. Years had been squandered as she hoped and wished she'd see him again. Finally, she realized she'd have only Ryan's broken promises to show for those lost years. Well, broken promises and her son.

She'd finally faced facts. There had been no word from the man she'd given her virginity to, no indication if he lived or had died or if he'd simply lost the desire to be part of her life. *Bastard!* Abby pushed herself up on to her feet and swiped at her tear-streaked face, determined to do the only thing guaranteed to make her forget. She started to clean. Not caring that she still had on her bridesmaid gown, she pulled out her cleaning supplies and got to work.

Her sisters had called to check on her, and concern had laced their voices. They had gone so far as to threaten to come over. Abby wouldn't let that happen, they didn't need to see the sad state she was in. What she'd let that man do to her again. She wanted to be alone to sort through her thoughts. Emma's reception wouldn't be ruined because of her. Abby insisted she was okay, only tired, and promised to call them in the morning. An assurance she wasn't looking forward to keeping. Abby had bought herself at least one more day to come to terms with the latest twists life had thrown her way.

She scrubbed the floors, countertops, and fixtures until everything shined. She cleaned her room and John's, dusting and vacuuming until there was nothing left to clean. Even the vent above the stove was shining underneath. She cleaned everything she could think of in an attempt not to think about the void he had left in her heart, a hole that might never truly mend. She collapsed on the couch and blew the hair out of her face, too tired to lift her arms she closed her eyes.

****

His mother lay asleep on the couch. The scent of chemicals filled the air, and John knew what she had been doing. What she always did when something bothered her—she cleaned. He'd seen her do it numerous times over the last eighteen years, mostly because of him.

His mom was the bravest person he knew. Hell, she caught criminals for a living for god's sake. She provided for and raised him when he knew the task hadn't always easy. He hated seeing her like this, and would be damned if he let that man do it to her again.

Emma and Jake had found him at the reception and warned him his father was in town. Flesh and blood or not, there was no way he was letting that man near her again. He could see, though, the damage had already done. She lay there exhausted, probably trying to banish the man from her thoughts. He ran his hand through his hair and let out a sigh before he scooped up her petite body and carried her to her room.

Her eyes fluttered open when John started to cover her with a blanket, and she whispered, "John?"

"Yeah, Mom, it's just me."

"Did they tell you?"

"Yeah, they did. Go back to sleep and we'll talk about it in the morning." He kissed her forehead and tucked her in, just as she had done for him his entire life.

"I'm so sorry, baby." The words slipped passed her lips before sleep consumed her again. John gently closed her door and went to his own room, exhausted from the wedding he crawled into bed and fell asleep.

He tossed and turned as the dreams came. Visions of his mother crying in pain filled his head. He struggled to see who had caused the anguish in her eyes but couldn't see the man's face, only a pentagram tattooed on the arm that held her captive. The man John wanted to kill. Butch was there, just in his line of sight, lying unconscious on the floor while his mom struggled to free herself from the ropes, and then the man was gone.

John shot upright in bed. The sweat-soaked sheets tangled around his body. His heart raced as he looked around his room, remembering where he was. The dream had been so real, so vivid, it made him shake. *It was just a dream.*

****

Abby's eyes cracked open. Her head felt like it was going to explode. She winced when she lifted her sore hand to cover her eyes from the sun shining through her bedroom window. Okay, hitting Ryan had done a number on her hand, and between the crying, cleaning, and the tequila, it was no wonder her head was pounding. Who was she kidding? She had needed it, but the headache was a reminder of the new problems that had walked into her life last night. Abby snuggled under the blanket. The soft bed was too comfortable to leave. She stretched. The sudden movement made her head hurt more, and her hand throbbed, bringing her back to thoughts of Ryan. Memories flashed back from the night before. *Why is he here? Why now?* It didn't make sense, not after all these years.

A hot shower would clear her head. She slid her legs over the edge of her bed and padded to the bathroom. She glanced in the mirror and grimaced. Her swollen red eyes were going to be hell to hide from her son. The warm water sluiced down her body, easing her aches and clearing her head. Her mind shifted from the man who had eluded her for so many years to the man who was probably already waiting in the kitchen. She dried off and dressed for the new day. One that didn't include Ryan.

Her stomach churned when she spotted the eggs. She held back the bile that threatened to rise in her throat, went straight for the coffee, and slid down into the chair. John placed a plate of toast and a bag of ice in front of her.

"The toast is for your stomach, and the ice is for your hand. Uncle Mike said you sure decked him good." John smiled his approval.

Kate Allenton

"John, I shouldn't have hit him. I should have just walked away. Some example I am."

John placed his hand on her shoulder and gave a gentle squeeze. "It's okay, Mom. I get it."

Abby glanced down at the table, unable to look her son in the eyes. "No, John, I was wrong."

"Mom, it's okay, really... We all understand." John moved around the table to stand across from her.

She had a vague memory of a brief conversation with her son the night before. She glanced up to find him staring at her. "Did you talk to him?"

"Nope, I don't have anything to say to the guy. He was just a sperm donor as far as I'm concerned. Hell, we don't even know his name."

"John, he's your father. It's okay if you want to get to know him. Just please understand that I can't." This was going to be harder on him. She had proved she had the strength deep down inside to live for eighteen years despite his deceit. Abby had never dreamed her son would have to deal with what this might mean to him.

"He's not my father. He doesn't even know about me. He wasn't here for me. He didn't raise me. He's nothing to me, only you mean something to me." John's tone was defiant. She truly expected him to stomp to his room and slam the door, like she'd seen him do numerous times in his younger days. The man who stood in front of her proved her wrong. He was no longer a child. He stood before her with his shoulders pulled back, chin held high and his arms crossed over his chest.

Abby released a breath she didn't know she'd been holding. This was going to be more difficult than any case she'd ever tried to solve. The events unfolding now affected her family, not an unknown victim. John needed to know his dad. Abby would never interfere with him forming a bond with the man. Assuming they found out his real name first.

She pushed away from the table, stood, then sipped her coffee. The hot liquid felt good going down her parched throat and helped clear her head. When John sat down and started eating his own eggs, Abby leaned over and kissed him on the head. "Thanks for the coffee, baby. I need to get to work, and we'll talk about this later."

They both were going to have to figure out how to deal with this in their own way.

CHAPTER 6

Abby arrived in the underground parking garage right on time. Butterflies danced in the pit of her stomach. She didn't relish the thought of the guys in the department having witnessed her breakdown at the wedding. She wasn't looking forward to them finding ways to pick one her and knew the jokes were about to begin. Mike stood propped against his undercover patrol car, waiting patiently for her to park. She released a sigh, not wanting the lecture she thought might be coming. Her plan was to walk past him and

Kate Allenton

pretend as though nothing had happened the night before, but he placed a gentle touch on her arm, stopping her in mid stride.

"I didn't do anything."

She smiled at her brother. "I don't want to talk about it. I just want to put it all behind me." She headed for the elevator with Mike by her side.

He pushed the button to call the elevator and turned to her. "I need to tell you something." His downward glance and the hesitation in his voice meant she wasn't going to like whatever it was that he had to say.

"Just spill it." She crossed her arms over her chest, tapping her foot, waiting for the roof to collapse. It couldn't be any worse than the night before.

"Abby, he's here in an official capacity. The captain said some agents with the FBI showed up last night, asking questions about your case, so he told them where to find you. He's not here about you or John, he's here about the murder."

That was it. Abby didn't think her heart could handle anymore. He wasn't even here to see her. She felt like such a flake. Of course, that's why he was here. It had been eighteen years, and he hadn't once tried to find her. Why would he choose now to pop back into her life? A bit hard on the ego, but maybe she could deal with him professionally and keep him at arm's length. *I should have known better.*

She turned to her brother and pasted a fake smile on her face. "Of course he is."

"Abby, you don't have to do this. I'll back you up with the captain. It doesn't have to be you." Mike followed her into the waiting elevator.

"We don't even know what he wants. Maybe he just wants to look at the evidence. If we're lucky, he'll be gone tomorrow," Abby said as she latched onto Mike's arm and laid her head against it, thankful he was such a good big brother.

She made it all the way to her office before her captain called her into the meeting. She knew who'd be

Kate Allenton

in there. Since Mike had talked with the captain last night, she guessed the proverbial cat had been let out of the bag, and she imagined she had some explaining to do. The butterflies assaulting her belly were now doing summersaults as she gave herself a pep talk.

"You can do this. He doesn't mean anything to you. You can do this." She repeated the mantra as she made her way to the captain's office. At least her brother had told her why Ryan was here, and not let her embarrass herself again by assuming it personal. That thought was what she clung too. She stopped with her hand on the doorknob, drew in a deep breath, and exhaled before pushing into the office.

The captain's office was big, well, maybe not with the three of them in it. The male bodies made it appear smaller than Abby had always felt it to be; the space they took up seemed to have shrunk it. Tension and testosterone filled the air, smacking her in the face when she entered. The hair on the back of her nape prickled as she made her way in and took an empty seat.

"Thanks for coming, Abby. I would like to introduce you to Sam Bennett," the captain said, motioning to the man she had wanted to avoid. Ryan stood next to her captain's desk, with his feet spread apart and hands shoved into the pockets of his black slacks. He hadn't taken his eyes off her, watching her every step. Maybe it was hard for him to have to ask for help, especially from her.

You have got to be kidding. Sam Bennett. Really? Abby couldn't contain herself. She threw her head back, and laughter erupted from her lips without warning. She didn't even try to contain it. Whether from nerves or the humor of the situation, she was unable to stop and unable to catch her breath. Tears trickled down her face as she swiped at them with the back of her hand.

"Did you check his ID? I'm sure we aren't missing a relative," she said, unable to stop smiling. She tried to even her breathing, taking deep breaths to control the laughter that still brimmed. Be professional, she reminded herself. *Aw hell, it's too late for that*

"I've seen the credentials, and after Mike told me your family knew him as Ryan, I called and verified them too," her Captain said as if that would make everything okay.

She stood and approached *Sam.* Her laughter was gone, only embarrassment and hurt remained, and that was simmering into raw fury as the seconds ticked by. She tilted her head to the side, narrowed her eyes, and asked, "Who are you really? Eighteen years ago when we met, your name was Ryan Douglas, and now you're Sam Bennett? How convenient for you. Do you take on everyone's last name you screw over?" Abby's voice rose with anger before she turned and stomped out the room, leaving all three men with their mouths hanging open.

She wasn't quick enough to make it back to her office alone. *Sam Bennett* was on her heels. The captain might reprimand Abby over her stunt, but really, it was something that had needed to be said, and so she had. Consequences be damned.

"Abby, wait! I can explain," Sam said as he grabbed her arm in an attempt to stop her. She stopped in her tracks, looking down at the hand on her arm, not turning to face the man she had cared for so many years before.

She had warned him the night before not to touch her. Her blood boiled from the audacity of this man as he waltzed in to ruin her life yet again. Her shoulders tensed, she grabbed hold of his hand, twisting until she maneuvered her weight just right and tossed him over her shoulder. With a thud, he landed sprawled out on the floor face up in front of her. All of those years taking defensive classes had paid off. A smile curved her lips. No, he didn't know her at all. She leaned over his body so he could see her face.

"Last night I warned you not to touch me. Don't do it again." She stepped over his body and made her way back to her office. Before she could shut her door, Matt jammed his foot over the threshold, making her unable to push it closed. *Not now.* She let out a long sigh and stalked to her window, wishing she hadn't even got out of bed this morning. Not even the serene landscape she had grown to love could soothe her frayed nerves.

"What was that about, Abby? Do you need me to take care of him?"

Her lips twitched, trying to hide the smile that threatened. That was one thing she could count on. When one of them had a problem, they all took on the responsibility of finding a solution. He placed his hands on her arms and gently rubbed them from behind. She was tempted to lean back into his embrace for the sheer comfort he offered, but thought it better not to lead him on. Her door opened, and "Sam" stomped in, coming to an abrupt halt.

"I'm sorry," he said. His gaze moved from Abby's face to Matt's and back again to land on her. His jaw twitched, he arched a brow, and then ran his hand through his brown hair, the same hair she'd touched so many times that summer. "Abby, I need thirty minutes with you. If, after that, you still don't want to work with me, I'll figure this out on my own. All I need is for you to listen."

Abby crossed her arms around her midsection as she stepped out of Matt's comforting embrace. Matt crossed his arms over his massive chest, the sleeves of his shirt were stretching tight, and his lips pulled into a thin line as he glared at Sam. "I don't think she wants you here, asshole."

Sam's eyes never left hers, ignoring Matt's comment all together. "I'm after the same guy you are. I've been chasing him for years. Besides, I heard you're the best at what you do, and with you on our team, we might actually have a chance to catch him this time. Abby, this guy isn't going to stop. He's going to continue to keep killing until we put him behind bars."

Abby knew that helping him would be a mistake, possibly a grave one, even though she was the logical choice. She could help him with his case and get him out of town even quicker, keeping her sanity and putting a killer away in the process. Abby lightly caressed Matt's arm. "It's all right, Matt. He's here about my case and nothing more. Right, *Sam*?" Her gaze landed on Ryan, her head tilted to the side, waiting for an answer she could live with. Her mind went back to the scene from two days ago. That's what she wanted to be focusing on, not either of the men occupying her office.

"I'll agree to that... for now," he said glaring at Matt. The testosterone-filled air thickened from their macho display. *I need some air.* She wanted out of the office and away from prying eyes. They needed to talk, but it couldn't happen here. No, she couldn't get away with hurting him without everyone watching her every move now that she had dumped him on his butt once. They would be keeping a closer eye on her, and some men in the department might end up getting in trouble by stepping in thinking she needed the help, just like Matt had done.

She pulled her gun from her holster, checked her ammo then shoved the clip back in and loaded a bullet in the chamber. Not as a display of power, hell, he probably had one bigger. She never left home without her piece hidden somewhere within reach, not since the lunatic with the knife had chased her and her sister, trying to kill them several months ago. Since then, all the men in the station had taken it upon themselves to appoint themselves as her protector. The Bennett women had inherited an extended family in the aftermath of the ordeal.

"Tell the captain he can reprimand me later. Sam and I are heading to the coroner's office." She left them standing there, unsure if Sam was going to follow her or not. She confidently continued on, out of her office toward the elevators. Her heartbeat sped up. She could feel his eyes on her, but she refused to give him the satisfaction of glancing back.

CHAPTER 7

Sam opened the passenger door and climbed into her SUV without invitation, folding his muscular body into the leather seat "You sure you don't want me to drive?" he said as he pulled the lever releasing the seat back as far as it would go. His gaze caressing her body sent a shiver down her spine as she buckled her belt.

"Nope, I'm good. You can always follow me if you'd rather drive yourself." She bit her lip. His presence in such tight quarters unnerved her. She inhaled a deep breath. He smelled of natural springs and everything right.

"No this is fine." He grabbed his belt, pulling it across his crisp white dress shirt to click in place.

Her phone rang, as she turned the key in the ignition. She hit the speaker button on the Bluetooth.

"Bennett," she said as she glanced at Sam, remembering his "new" last name and shook her head. Yes, she would have to remember to ask him about that one, she'd been waiting until they were alone. She couldn't fathom why he would be using her last name. She rolled her eyes and wondered if he would actually tell her the truth or feed her more lies, like he'd done eighteen years ago.

"Abby, are you all right?" her sister Emma asked. *This can't be good.* If Emma was asking, she must be getting one her "special" feelings again or Momma Mae made her call. That was Emma's gift—she saw dead people, well, only one dead person anyway, Momma Mae, a ghost that refused to show herself to anyone but Emma and now her new hubby, Jake. Her other gift was the PMS-like symptoms she would get when one of her family members was in trouble, and for her to be calling with that question left little doubt in Abby's mind something was wrong. She needed to warn Emma, she wasn't alone and stop her before she said something that might expose their secret. That was the reason behind the warning system they'd created years ago.

She let out a sigh. "I've had better days, but it's nothing a little chocolate couldn't cure." She emphasized chocolate and prayed her sister remembered their code, another one of her family's way to keep their secret safe. Chocolate, the easiest for all three girls to remember because it was a favorite, meant they couldn't speak freely, but they were fine. Pecans were used to tell the others they were fine but should probably stay away from the house.

Mike never liked when his sisters used the code because, as they were growing up, he was never sure if the warning was because of a boy or an actual problem. Lemons, meant trouble, the call-the-police kind of trouble and get them here quick.

The last code word was the most severe. If the words were ever muttered, everyone scattered to a prearranged destination, having no contact until they'd all met up together. They hadn't had to use the last one yet but had instituted it just in case for emergencies.

There wasn't a chance in hell any of their family members would be confused by this request. They'd came up with a code word that was avoided like the plague but still subtle enough not to attract the kind of attention that one of them screaming, "run for your life" would bring. *Broccoli*. There wasn't a member of their family that could stomach the green veggie.

"How about I bring you some later unless you need Jake to bring you some now?" Emma asked. Concern filled her voice. The offer to send her big bodyguard husband meant she still remembered the code and was concerned for her safety.

"That won't be necessary, Em. But I'll call if that changes."

"Yeah, well, I think I'm going to have to send him to the store for some Midol, anyway, if this niggling of a headache doesn't go away." That was Emma's way of warning her that trouble loomed close for her or one of the family members. Lord knew Emma sure didn't need the stuff, not when she was two months pregnant and expecting her first baby. She smiled at her sister's coded message, but her heart raced at the thought of one of them being in trouble. She wiped her sweaty palms on her pants. They needed to be on the lookout, and that changed her plans.

"Make sure you call everyone if the headache doesn't go away. I'm sure one of us can pick up the medicine and bring it over to you, including John." The trouble might be for one of them instead, and she didn't want to take any chances.

She ended the call and glanced at her passenger. "Sorry, you know how sisters are." She shrugged her shoulders. "Well, come to think of it,

Kate Allenton

I'm not so sure you do." Remembering that she didn't really know him at all, she continued to drive toward the parking exit. Her mind raced, trying to figure out what could be wrong. She would need to be able to talk to Emma without prying ears to see if there was more to the message, maybe more that Momma Mae could fill her in on.

She pulled out of the garage, glancing in the rearview mirror, and she caught the tail immediately. The silver glint on the SUV following her in the hot North Carolina sun was hard to miss. She chanced a quick glance at Sam and clenched the steering wheel so hard it turned her knuckles white. She wasn't sure what tipped off Sam, whether it was her death grip on the wheel or her constant glance in the rearview mirror. She took a few unscheduled turns and weaved in and out of traffic, putting distance between them and their tail. She concentrated only on getting away from the car that was speeding to keep up. She maneuvered through the streets, passing the familiar buildings, people and cars she'd seen every day since starting her job at the precinct. She whispered her silent thanks that she'd lived in this town all her life and knew these roads, as well as every nook and cranny, like the back of her hand.

She had put several car lengths between her and their shadow, enough to swerve into another parking garage and park next to a black SUV similar to hers. Minutes ticked by, and the silver SUV hadn't found them. She stayed in her hiding place. It might have been her imagination, but she wasn't taking any chances, not since Emma had been run off the road and almost killed. She hadn't noticed Sam on the phone or listened in to his conversation, but she saw him disconnecting the call. His eyes trained on the garage entrance. When she was sure they had lost the car, she put her car in park and let her hands drop to her lap as she blew her bangs out of her eyes.

Kate Allenton

"You okay?" he asked as he reached for her hand.

His grip wasn't tight, but comforting, a familiar touch she remembered from years ago. His touch sent a spark through her system. She closed her eyes and soaked in his comfort. His touch elicited a vision of unfamiliar images behind her closed eyes. Grief hit her senses, strong enough to make her almost choke. She wasn't sure if the feelings were his or hers. Abby hadn't been able to pick up on feelings before; images were the only thing her gift normally gave her. *This is something new*. Her muscles tensed. Then the loneliness took hold, bringing an unshed tear to her eye. Was it possible Sam had been as miserable as she'd been all these years?

All of the intense emotions she experienced drained from her body, as foreign images filled her mind from his touch. The younger version of Sam had crouched behind a car when startled by the sound of a woman's blood-curdling scream through a moonlit sky. A man ran from the house in a hurry leaving the door wide open in his haste. She zeroed in on the only physical description that held her captive from the man fleeing the scene. The lighted street revealed a pentagram, tattooed on his left arm, and it was identical to the one above her victim's bed without the initials RD. *Ryan Douglas,* she thought. Abby watched as the scared young boy shivered, before standing and in his curiosity crossed the street entering the house. Abby wanted to follow. She needed to know what lay beyond the open door, but just as sudden as she appeared to witness the event, she was pulled back to her world.

"Abby, are you alright?" Sam asked, now squeezing her hand.

Her gift had given her a glimpse of what had happened all of those years ago to the man sitting beside her.

She gasped, opened her eyes, and pulled her hand from his. She knew why he was here, he had told her the truth, and now her gift

Kate Allenton

confirmed it. Uncertainty hit her. He was after the same killer she was. *We need to catch this guy.*

She gazed into his eyes. "Sorry." She cleared her throat. "I'm fine. Did you get a look at the driver?" Her mind was spinning in several directions as she tried to process all of the information. She needed to figure him out, fast, if she had any hope of getting through this with her heart intact. She needed her sister Claire. Claire could read thoughts if she concentrated hard enough. Abby would make it a point to get him near Claire in the extremely near future. For now, she decided to go for the honest approach and just ask. She'd use Claire as a last resort, her ace in the hole to validate what Sam said was true.

She closed her eyes once more, unable to look in his blue eyes, and drew in a breath, inhaling his earthy musk that filled the car. She opened her eyes and turned in her seat. "You're here because of the pentagram, aren't you?"

"Yes."

She peered out her window into the vast darkness of the garage. "You really do know who this guy is, don't you? He put your initials in the middle of it so you'd come here." She said it more as a statement than a question. Her heart was breaking again. It confirmed he truly hadn't come here for her.

His lack of response told her what she needed to know. She put the car in reverse and backed out of their alcove. Her mind was reeling, trying to analyze this new piece of information.

His voice pulled her from her thoughts. "Abby, we need to go somewhere so we can talk," he explained calmly. She knew he was right. She would need to try to put everything behind them to catch this guy before he killed again, and she needed to tell him about his son. What happened between them would have to wait to be dealt with. Her son and catching this asshole would have to come first.

She glanced his way for a brief second before training her eyes on

Kate Allenton

the road again. "We're heading to the morgue right now, but tonight you can bring the files you have on this guy over to my house and we'll talk." She hit the button for the radio, ending any further conversation. Telling him about John would be the hardest thing she'd ever have to do.

CHAPTER 8

The visit to the morgue hadn't told them any more than they already knew, except that the abrasions around her neck weren't from a rope and were inflicted postmortem. Matt was back at the office, processing some of her evidence in an attempt to get Sam out of her life. He was sending the blood off for DNA testing to be run through the national security database and had the rest of her department helping out too. *He's so sweet.*

Kate Allenton

Abby had dropped Sam off at the precinct and left him there. Her mind was fuzzy with everything that had happened. She wasn't going to be able to concentrate today even though this work needed her full concentration, and her heart was busy trying to decide what to do about Sam. She needed the only other thing that had kept her sane for the last eighteen years. She needed the company of her sisters, specifically Emma.

Abby parked on Main Street across from the Starlight Café, her sister's pride and joy. She wasn't sure if Emma was working today, especially after the wedding, but it was worth a shot. Abby hesitated, closing her eyes, and said a silent prayer for strength before pushing open her car door.

Biting her lip, oblivious to her surroundings, she crossed the street, her mind clouded with thoughts of Sam and how to tell him the truth about John.

Abby noticed her sister's VW bug parked out front and pushed through the doors. The sweet smell of coffee hit her nose as she bypassed the full tables. *Business is good*, she thought to herself and smiled. Emma deserved it. An outcast from an early age, Emma had the worst time out of all of her family trying to hide her gifts and acting like a normal kid. Her heart swelled, and a grin teased her lips when she saw her pregnant sister. Emma was talking to a table full of little old ladies—the town gossips—that frequented the place. Everyone wondered how the women knew everything they did. Now that her sister had settled down with Jake, they had turned their attention on her, trying to set her up on blind dates. All of them had a nephew or a friend of the family that would be perfect for her, and they told her every chance they got.

She would have avoided Mrs. Anderson if Emma hadn't been talking to her. Mrs. A was a very old, wise woman, even a pleasure to talk to when she wasn't trying to play matchmaker. Abby ordered and grabbed her coffee from the counter

Kate Allenton

as she made her way over to the table. She took a sip of the steaming liquid and burned her tongue in the process. Par for the course, she thought. Her day seemed to be going down hill. Thank god, her sister hadn't left for her honeymoon right away. Being short handed during the tourist season and Jake's move of his company had postponed their trip.

"Hey, Abby." Emma grinned with a gleam in her eyes. "We were just talking about you." Amusement flickered in her eyes. She was enjoying this.

Abby glared at her sister. Emma must have a perverse pleasure in watching her squirm. "Emma." She smirked and then smiled at Mrs. A. "What was the topic this time? Is it the case I'm working on?" Abby asked.

"Well, no dear, we did hear about it, but we have faith you'll catch the bad guy. You always do, dear. We were talking about finding you a man," the little old lady said with a big smile. Her dentures were as white as her tight curled hair.

Silence filled the air. Abby's gaze took in the rest of the diners. The locals apparently wanted to hear this conversation as much as Abby didn't want to have it.

Abby's shoulders slumped as she lowered her head before lifting it again toward the little old lady, resigned she wasn't going to get out of having this conversation. Abby lifted her chin. "I appreciate that, Mrs. A, but I don't need a man." Abby gave a gentle squeezed to her hand.

She knew the old lady meant well but didn't have the energy to debate it with her. Not today. Mrs. A must have sensed Abby's defeat, but she didn't skip a beat. Abby glanced at Emma. Her sister shrugged and held her hands palm out, making it evident she hadn't played a part in all of this.

"Oh dear, we know you don't want a man. You've told us so numerous times. But well, we know what happened at the wedding, and that man isn't right for you."

"What man are you talking about?" Abby couldn't stop the words that flew from her mouth; she knew which man but just wanted to forget. She took another sip of coffee in an attempt to keep her mouth occupied before she said something she couldn't take back. The scalding liquid burned going down her throat, as she waited for her answer. She would need the energy later to deal with Ryan, no, Sam, she reminded herself.

"The man you hit at Emma's reception, dear. You need someone that can protect you, and from the looks of him last night, I don't think he's the one for you."

Abby gasped, putting her hand over her mouth to stop the coffee from spewing from her lips, choking to get the rest of the warm liquid down her throat. Emma laughed. Her laughter drew attention from the patrons sitting nearby. They didn't even know who he was, much less that he was probably capable of far more than protecting her. The old ladies at the table looked at each other, shrugged, and stared at her, waiting for a reply.

She straightened and wiped the coffee from her chin. She hadn't expected the news to travel so fast. Abby patted Mrs. A on the shoulder. "You have no idea."

"But, of course I do, dear. That's John's dad. He's the spitting image of that man." The truth stopped them all from laughing.

Her eyes widened with alarm, and she turned to look at her sister. Little good all of her education had done. She should have been smart enough to realize he might find out from someone other than her. She needed to tell him before the rest of the town spilled the beans. Her heart raced as she glanced at her watch, the same diamond studded watch Jake had made for all of them as gifts for the wedding. The delicate white gold watch with diamonds told her that she still had time before he showed up at her house.

"Mrs. A..." She wasn't sure what she was going to say. She felt the blood rush from her face.

Kate Allenton

"Don't worry, dear. We aren't going to tel him. Anywho, there is a man I want you to meet. He's new to town and renting my cabin, and boy, is he a looker. He's a bit older than you but a very nice man and pays his rent on time." Mrs. A toyed with the locket around her neck. It vaguely reminded Abby of the one she'd seen in her vision from the crime scene days before.

"That's a beautiful locket, Mrs. A. Where did you get it?"

"Oh thank you dear, it was a gift from my new renter. He's nice to old ladies, Abby. I'm sure he'd be good for you to, if you just gave him a chance."

"I'm sorry, Mrs. A. I've got too much on my plate right now, dealing with Ryan." Abby shook her head. "I mean Sam and this murder. Maybe another time." She grabbed her sister by the elbow and steered her toward her office in the back of the building.

She took a glance over her shoulder and smiled at the old lady. "It was nice talking to you," she said, lying through her teeth to the woman. Her lips tilted up, and she felt a blush rising to her cheeks. *That's what I get for living in a small town.*

Emma stepped into her office and sat behind her desk. Abby collapsed in a chair and exhaled as she watched her sister shuffle the papers out of the way. Emma was positively glowing. She was only two months pregnant and didn't have a baby bump yet, but her eyes sparkled and her skin glowed. Emma smiled a lot more since meeting her husband. Abby hadn't seen her sister this happy in a long time. Come to think of it, she'd never seen her sister this happy.

Abby hesitated, unsure whether she wanted to get into the hard conversation just yet and upset her pregnant sister, so she decided on another topic, the same topic that had put the sparkle in her sister's eyes. She asked, "Where's Jake?"

"He's at the hanger, checking his planes that came in today. He's finally done moving the business here. The planes were the last of it."

Her brother-in-law owned Tactical Maneuvers, a prestigious security and bodyguard firm in Virginia. He'd been on vacation and had been pulled into Emma's stalker situation. Since then they'd fallen in love. He'd moved his business here to ensure her happiness and brought most of his employees too. Reminding Abby that Butch was now a permanent fixture in her life gave her a reason to smile. Abby would never be able to repay the strength that man gave her. He was like her brother, but with a sense of humor.

"He's getting one of them ready for the trip to the beach house."

"You aren't using one of ours?" Abby asked. She had never really thought he might own his own fleet of planes, but it made sense. He was loaded, and it was easier for him to send his bodyguards and security personnel out across the country when he needed to instead of buying plane tickets. She and her siblings each had their own planes. Their father had left them a whole fleet, and they all knew how to fly them, including John. Flying was the one thing that had made her dad happy. It was convenient when they took their summer trips down to the beach every year. If broccoli was ever muttered by one of them, it would eventually get them to their final meeting place at the beach house. The one place she would never forget.

"What brings you by?" Her sister's voice pulled her from her thoughts.

"His new name is Sam Bennett."

"Wait a minute. I thought his name was Ryan." Emma drew her brows together and folded her hands on her desk.

Abby closed her eyes, took a deep breath, and leaned her head back against the top of the leather chair. Her stomach still fluttered from her brief encounter with Sam that morning. Her sister would help her figure this out. Her family was her rock. They kept her grounded and had always been there for her when she needed them.

"The man we know as Ryan, apparently changed his name to Sam

Bennett." After the words had left her mouth, she raised her head to look at Emma.

"I'm not sure I understand, Who goes around changing their name like that, and why the hell did he pick Bennett!" Emma said as she stood and put her hands on her hips, with a scowl on her face. Her eyes darkened with emotion, and she cocked her head to the side.

"That's good, because I don't understand either." She gazed up at her sister.

"Please sit back down, Emma, so I can tell you the rest." Emma sat back down in her chair, her demeanor stiff.

"There's more?"

"Yeah, I'm surprised Mike hasn't called you about it. I kind of dumped him on his ass when he grabbed my arm." Abby raised her eyebrow and bit her bottom lip.

Abby could see some of the tension leave Emma's body when she leaned back in the chair, more relaxed, and smiled before replying, "Good."

"He needs my help on a case, and he's bringing me his files tonight," Abby admitted. She sat dazed, her stomach completing summersaults. How could she still be attracted to a guy that had lied to her about something so important?

"I'm not sure that's a good idea, Abby. Why can't you meet here at the café? Or at least in public," her sister said as she rounded the desk and sat in the leather chair next to Abby's.

"I need to tell him, Emma, and I'd rather do it in private. I'm going to tell him about John." She studied the invisible lint on her pants, unable to look her sister in the eyes. Disappointment from her family would kill her if they didn't think she was making the right choice. She felt eighteen again, having to admit that a summer fling had resulted in pregnancy. She had fallen hard for the teenager next door. She'd been stunned when they tried to find him to tell him about the baby to find out he hadn't even given her the correct name. A cloud of embarrassment hovered over her head.

She squirmed in her seat as she twisted her hands that now lay in her lap. She felt Emma place her hand on hers, stopping her movement. She lifted her gaze, and her eyes found her sister's. All she saw reflected back was love and sympathy. Emma squeezed her hand. "I'm proud of you."

Tears swelled in her eyes and threatened to fall as Abby swallowed the lump in her throat. "You are?" she asked, unsure she'd heard her right.

"You are the strongest woman I know, Abby Bennett, and I'm proud you're my sister. No matter what happens, we'll get through this," Emma assured her as a tear escaped and trickled down her face. Emma pulled her into an embrace and hugged her tight while whispering in her ear. "Mom and Dad would have been so proud of you, Abby."

Abby leaned back and searched her sister's eyes. Emma's smile never wavered as another tear escaped. Abby pushed herself up from the chair and walked to the door with new determination to do the right thing and be a better person than Sam had been all of those years before. She just needed to find the right words to tell him. Emma's pep talk hadn't calmed her nerves, but it had provided the strength she needed to get through this.

She smiled, let out a shaky breath, and turned to her older sister. "Thanks, Emma."

"Abby, we aren't leaving for the beach house until tomorrow afternoon, just in case you need me."

CHAPTER 9

Abby drove to her house on autopilot. She hadn't noticed the scenery as she tried to run the conversations she needed to have in her mind. Dread filled her thoughts, making her shudder. The conversation she needed to have with Sam consumed her mind. Her attention wasn't focused on her surroundings. She had zoned out, her mind reeling with potential scenarios of how her conversation would go. She chewed the inside of her cheek, and her pulse quickened the closer she got to her house. She pulled out her phone.

She punched in the familiar number for her son, who answered on the second ring.

"Hey, Mom."

"Hey, John, I just wanted to warn you that Sam is coming over to the house tonight to bring me some files and so we can talk." Abby was almost certain he wouldn't want to be at the house, nevertheless, she would do the right thing and ultimately make it his decision.

"Who's Sam?" John asked.

Abby's lips tilted. "Your dad."

"Are you sure that's his name? How do you know he isn't lying?"

"He's with the FBI and is only here about my investigation. The captain introduced us today. I'm not sure why he changed his name, but I'm going to find out."

"Did you tell him about me?" John's voice cracked. Abby didn't know what to make of the uncertainty in her son's voice.

"I'm telling him tonight. Do you want to meet him?"

"Nope and I really wish you wouldn't have anything to do with him. Mom, I don't want you to get hurt by that bastard."

"John, I'm not going to let him hurt me, and after I tell him about you, you can't let that stand in the way of getting to know him." She didn't want her son to get hurt by Sam's reaction to finding out he has a kid, and right now she didn't know what to expect. Abby needed to make it clear to John that, should he want to meet the man, she wouldn't stand in the way.

"I'm at Emma's with Butch. Call me after he leaves, and I'll come home."

"Okay, baby, I'll call you later."

Abby wished she could have had that conversation face to face to gauge his expressions, but she didn't want him surprised if Sam had shown up while he was there. She wasn't going to keep anything from John, not when it concerned his dad.

Abby pulled onto her street and slowed her vehicle to a roll when she spotted Sam sitting on her steps. He'd changed into jeans and a t-shirt with his shoulder holster securely strapped to his arms. His shoulders were hunched, and he had his head hanging low toward the ground with his arms propped on his legs. His chestnut hair looked disheveled, like he had run his hands through it several times. He must be dreading the upcoming conversation as much as she was.

The butterflies in her stomach were still having their own

marathon, but she wasn't going to put it off, no matter what the outcome was. The road construction had prevented him from parking in her drive, and it seemed she wouldn't be able to park there either.

"Just great," she mumbled under her breath. She wouldn't even get a chance to relax. The orange safety cones not only blocked her drive but everyone's yard. She wasn't the only one inconvenienced by the county's improvement plans. She pulled in behind a black SUV across the street from her house and unbuckled her seatbelt. The SUV was a replica of the one she drove. The only difference she noted was the out-of-state plate. *Virginia. Maybe I should run the tag.*

She slowed her breathing to steady the rhythm of her erratic heartbeat, and reached quickly for the door handle before she lost her nerve She focused on Sam, who now stood on her porch with a partial grin. The screeching of tires broke the connection between them, and her eyes jerked to the silver SUV speeding in her direction. Abby panicked and froze in the gutter in front of her house White smoke rose from the tires as the driver pushed harder on the gas. Everything seemed to slow down. She heard her cell ringing and Sam screaming but couldn't make out what he was saying. At the last minute, she tried to jump out of the way and dive toward the grass, but it wasn't fast enough. Several things happened at once. Sam was running toward her with his weapon drawn, and the next thing she knew, her body, along with some of the orange cones, was airborne. Her stomach rose to her throat before she hit the fluffy grass in her yard with a thud. The impact knocked the wind from her lungs as her head bounced off the hard ground.

She struggled to pull in a breath, rolling onto her side. Intense pain radiated up her leg and the need to close her eyes threatened. She swallowed hard, gasping. Abby heard a gunshot and tried to lift her head but couldn't focus so she laid her head back down. She had expected to see the little tweety birds flying around in a circle above her head. She felt soft hands lift her head. It hurt to keep her eyes open, the pain making it almost unbearable. She gritted her teeth and tried to open her eyes. She looked up, and her gaze locked with Sam's. An intensity she'd never seen before, shown in his eyes. He had his phone to his ear, and she couldn't make out the words passing over his lips. As her eyes fluttered

Kate Allenton

shut, she thought she heard Sam's deep voice, unsure if it was all in her head, saying, "I'm sorry, Abby, don't leave me." That was the last thing she remembered before her world went dark.

****

Abby realized she was no longer lying on her grass but on a soft bed. Cool sheets cocooned her body. She heard beeping sounds in the distance. A calloused hand held hers, and there was a soft pressure on her belly. Abby's eyes fluttered open. She looked down at the pressure. Sam had his head laid across her belly with his head turned toward her, staring at her face. His eyes brimmed with unshed tears.

"How do you feel?" His voice cracked as he lifted his head but held fast to her hand.

"Let's just say it hasn't been the best day of my life," Abby said, trying to lighten the mood, and watched him squirm in his seat. An unchecked tear dripped from his eyes, and he reached up and batted it away.

"I thought I lost you, baby." He leaned over and pressed his soft lips to her forehead. "I didn't think you were going to move."

Maybe she'd hit her head harder than she thought. That must be it. Why was he acting like he cared? This didn't make sense.

"I must've hit my head pretty hard," she said as she tried to move her legs. Her bones were stiff and sore. Pain radiated up her leg as she took a few deep breaths and pushed the sheet off of her to gauge the damage.

"Just bruising, no stitches." He reached for the sheet to help and placed his hand behind her back, gently helping her to sitting position. He pushed the button on the bed and rearranged her pillows.

"Anything broken?" she asked as she tried again to move her leg.

"No, baby. Thank god he just clipped you. If he hadn't swerved when you jumped out of the way, I'm not sure we'd be having this conversation." Memories of the accident flooded her mind; it was the same damn SUV. She should have been paying more attention and kept her eye on her surroundings as her family had taught her. She'd been so focused on the man waiting for her she hadn't realized the car was gunning straight for her until it was almost too late.

"It was the same SUV, wasn't it?" She tried to reach for the pitcher of water sitting on the table beside her bed, and couldn't get her fingers around it. He gently helped her rest back against the pillows and poured a cup for her. His fingers brushed hers, sending tingles down her arm. Heat flooded her core, and she was sure her heart skipped a beat as she looked into his eyes. No smile touched his lips, but she was trapped by his gaze. It was almost as if he were seeing deep down to her soul.

"I didn't see it, until the last minute, but I'm sure it was, unless someone else is trying to kill you. Listen, Abby, I need to tell you something, and this is as good a place as any, hell, maybe better. You can't run or throw a punch from where you're sitting." He smiled down at her.

"I guess I don't have a choice." Uncertainty assailed her. The flutter in her stomach did little to calm her nerves. Her heart beat erratically. This talk was going to change everything. She just didn't know if it was going to be for the better or the worse. She'd known the time was coming but had assumed she would be the one to bring it up.

"I'm sorry for everything, Abby. When I met you, my life had been turned upside down. I was the only witness to a murder and was in protective custody during his trial. He was acquitted. They believed that the jury was tampered with but couldn't prove it. I was only eighteen when they put me in the witness protection program. They changed my name and told me to have a nice life."

Her heart felt like it was being torn from her chest, but she now had confirmation of the scenes she'd seen from his touch. It made sense. She believed what he was telling her. A single tear she couldn't hold back trickled down her face. She couldn't imagine being uprooted from her family and having to start over with no one on her side.

The desire to comfort him took over. She took hold of his hand and gave it a gentle squeeze, and in a soft voice, whispered, "I'm sorry."

"I really did love you, Abby. We might have been young and only known each other for a month but don't doubt for a minute that I loved you. I was coming back to the beach house when Stone called me." Sam sat down on the bed careful of her leg and took her hands in his. Abby wanted to take all of his pain away and never let him go.

She closed her eyes and thought back all those years ago, trying to recall the name Stone. When nothing registered, she finally opened her eyes and asked, "Who?"

"He was the man pretending to be my father. He was the

federal agent assigned to protect me. He called and told me the judge had been killed and asked if we could meet." He pulled in a breath, and his eyes searched her face, though she didn't know what he was looking for. His gaze went from her eyes to her lips and back up again.

"I was coming back for you; I swear it. I met with Stone, and he talked some sense into me. I couldn't be selfish and put you and your family in danger. I had to wait until the bastard was caught."

"Oh, Sam, I'm so sorry. If I had known, we could have helped and protected you."

"Richard Daley got away with it. He killed that woman and now is suspected in the judge's murder too. We figured it was only a matter of time before he set his sights on me to tie up his loose ends."

She remained silent. His jaw clenched, his eyes slightly narrowed. His whole body tensed as if reliving it in his mind. He reached for her face, his palm cupping her cheek.

"He convinced me not to go back to you. Told me that, if I really loved you, I would need to be a man and walk away, at least for a while. Had I know that it was going to be eighteen years, I'm not sure I would have agreed with him. I knew he was right at the time, as much as I wanted to be with you, I couldn't bring this killer into your life. My plan was to join the military and learn to defend myself. I needed to be a stronger man, not just for myself, but for you."

She leaned forward and placed a gentle kiss on his lips. All this lost time they would never get back. Her heart tugged for the lost stolen years. He didn't even yet realize the extent of what he'd lost. He would never get back all the years he missed watching John grow up into a man. Her resolve strengthened. She needed to tell him. She leaned her forehead against his. "I wish you would've told me."

"I couldn't do that to you. I served my country, and it made me a better man. When I came back, I went to college, and then joined the FBI, and that was when he struck again, this time leaving a calling card. It's always the same."

The pieces finally came together. "The pentagram."

"Yep, he leaves the pentagram somewhere at the scene. I've made it my goal to catch the bastard. I couldn't let him follow me back to you, so I stayed away. The years passed, and by then, I figured I was too late. I assumed you had moved on. I still hadn't caught the guy, and I wouldn't risk it, Abby, I couldn't risk him finding out how much you mean to me."

Abby felt the walls she had built around her heart start to crumble. The butterflies assaulted her once again. She needed to tell him the truth, tell him about his son and give him back some of his stolen time with John.

"Sam, there's something I need to tell you..."

The door opened, and Dr. Lister sauntered in with her clipboard in hand. "Abby, I'm glad you're awake now."

She stopped in mid stride. Her gaze flicked from Abby to Sam and back. "Sorry I'm interrupting, but I really need to check your bruise and vitals." She made her way to the side of the bed.

"Sam, please don't leave. I have something important to tell you," she said as he stood from the bed and went to the window.

"I'm not going anywhere, baby," he said as he took a seat in the corner of the room, waiting patiently for the doctor to finish her checkup.

CHAPTER 10

"You Bennett girls really aught to invest in some helmets," the doctor joked as she removed the bandage covering her ugly bruise. The black, blue, and purple area spanned from the top of her thigh almost all the way down to her knee. She wouldn't be doing yoga anytime soon, hell, or running for that matter. The doctor applied some more stuff that looked like goop and redressed the area.

"At least you didn't end up with a concussion like Emma did," the doctor said as she placed the blood pressure cup around Abby's arm. "The crème will help reduce the inflammation, I'd suggest using a heating or cooling pad for the first 48 hours and stay off of it as much as possible."

"I'm okay, Doc. Are you going to release me?" The doc turned to look at Sam now stretching in a chair in the corner. His body too big for the small chair, he leaned back with his legs extended in front of him and his fingers laced behind his head. A smile curved his lips. Relief was evident in his posture, like the weight of the world had been lifted from his muscular shoulders.

Dr. Lister looked back at Abby. "You girls sure know how to pick them. We need to have lunch one day so you can tell me your secret," she whispered before she straightened.

"I'll go start the paperwork." She looked around the room "Where is your obnoxious brother? I assumed he'd already be here yelling and scaring the nurses," she said as she smiled.

The door burst opened. Mike stormed in and froze halfway through the door when he saw the good doc. His sudden stop made the people behind him bounce off his back. Emma hit him on the arm as she sidestepped her way past their brother. Abby's lips tilted up in the corners. The scowl on her brother's face should have been enough to scare the petite doctor, but it didn't. Emma, Jake, Claire, Butch, and John pushed passed Mike, bumping his shoulder as they passed to enter into her now too-small hospital room. Her eyes got big, and her jaw dropped when she saw her son.

"Shit," she muttered under her breath. Her gaze went from Sam to John and back again.

People were asking her questions, but her world narrowed to the two men that had consumed her life. Sam was now standing in front of his chair and had his gaze glued on their son. She watched in panic as they stared at each other. There was no denying the similarities between them. The room turned silent when everyone else turned to see what held her enthralled.

Abby cleared her dry throat. "Sam, I'd like you to meet John...our son." His eyes went from John's to hers, and Sam stepped closer. John held up his hand to stop his advance.

"Don't be confused, old man. I don't care who you are; you're nothing but a sperm donor to me, but let me warn you now. I want you to leave my mom alone. You've been in town for less then seventy-two hours and look where she is." He pointed to the hospital bed then clenched his fist. His face turned red as anger threatened to overtake him. She'd only seen her son like this once, over a girl, and she knew the outcome. Before any words could pass her lips, John advanced on Sam. Butch stepped between the two before John could come to blows and placed his hand on John's chest.

"Jonathan Mitchell, he can explain. And I taught you better manners than that, young man," she scolded from her bed. Unable to get up, she felt helpless in diffusing their first encounter. Her shoulders tightened as her hands clenched the sheet.

"This is all my fault," she whispered.

Butch turned to face John. "Look, man, she doesn't need this right now. Look around you." He waved to encompass the whole room. "Dude, think about your mom. She's hurt and doesn't need this on top of everything else."

John turned back to his mother, ignoring the older man. "I'm sorry, Mom." He stepped to her bed and kissed her head. She grabbed his hand and pulled him close. This wasn't going to be a quick fix. She leaned her head against his. "He's got a good reason, kid. Give him a chance."

John clenched his eyes closed and released a breath. "If you believe him, I'll try." That was the best response he could have given her. "When are they letting you out?"

Dr. Lister took that moment to diffuse the tension in the room. "In a few minutes, after I file a copy of her discharge paperwork." Dr. Lister held out the carbon copy of it in her hand. Sam took the paperwork from Dr. Lister who smirked at Mike, and sauntered out of the room with Mike hot on her heels.

John advanced on Sam and held out his hand. "I'll take those."

"I've got them, Junior." He folded and pocketed the papers.

John's jaw twitched, and Abby could see him grinding his teeth. He dropped his hand to his side. "You won't be here to take care of her. I will. Now hand them over." He bowed his chest, and narrowed his eyes. Abby silently wondered if John would come to blows with his father.

"So much for trying." Abby shook her head and rested it on the pillow.

"Kid...I'm not going anywhere." Sam crossed his arms over his chest as he gauged the faces in the room.

Abby felt that emotions were all over the place. Butch stood in an identical poise, as did most of the others. The tension made the hair on the back of her neck stand on ends. Testosterone filled the room. Damn men thought they were the bosses of her.

"She can't go back there. It isn't safe. He knows where she lives now. I'm taking her with me. I have just the place to keep her safe."

Her sisters let out a joint gasp. Butch stepped up, putting his hand against Sam's chest. "Like hell, buddy. We don't know you; she can stay with me. I'll protect her."

Her face felt red as she repositioned herself on the bed, adamant they were so not having this conversation without her. *Oh, hell no.* "I'm not going anywhere without John. He's not staying in that house until we find this asshole."

Emma repositioned the pillow behind Abby's back to make it more comfortable. It wasn't so long ago that she and Jake had been in this hospital. "You guys can come to the beach house with us, and you can stay at our house until we leave. You'll both be safe there, and we have plenty of room." She smiled, obviously trying to appease everyone and kill the mounting tension that soured the room. Emma glanced back at her new husband, who gave her a nod and placed his hand on her shoulder. The simple gesture loosened some of Abby's pent-up stress.

"John's going to stay with you." She took Emma's hand. "I need to help catch this guy so we can go home again, and Sam is the only one that can help me. He's been tracking this guy for a long time and knows his habits. I'm going to need his knowledge." She wouldn't be able to concentrate if John was in danger. That wasn't going to be an option.

"We'll take care of John." Emma leaned over and hugged her sister. I promise," Emma whispered in her ear as everyone in the room watched in silence.

Claire leaned over and hugged her too. She whispered in her other ear, "If you need me, I'm just a phone call away, and I'll come find you. I've got enough connections in this town, it wouldn't be hard. There aren't many places he can hide you. I can't get a read on him with so many people in the room, but I will, if you need me to."

Mike burst back in the room with the doctor trailing behind him. Her lips were swollen, and her hair a bit mused. She lifted her hand to her lips without taking her eyes off Mike. "What did I miss?" he asked as he searched the silent faces for clues.

Abby rolled her eyes, and Emma mumbled, "Everything," as she grabbed John's hand, pulling him behind her and Jake.

****

He arrived at the hospital after ditching the SUV and stealing another car. He hadn't meant to hurt the little spitfire, well, at least not yet. He'd just wanted to scare her. He

Kate Allenton

had plans for her, and it didn't include killing her just yet. He sauntered into the lobby, about to ask for a room number when a younger version of Ryan/now Sam was exiting with another couple. *Well, well, well, what do we have here?* It seemed Sam had been a very naughty boy and had produced an offspring. The young man was the spitting image of Ryan, when the little bastard had witnessed his crime eighteen years before. His direction changed, and he followed them out. *This just keeps getting better and better. This small town is just full of surprises, first the girl and now the kid.* He hadn't expected the bonus of both the spitfire and an offspring. Now it was just a choice of which would help him get to Sam.

He contemplated a new plan as he got in the car and followed the vehicle with the young man to a gated house. He hid his vehicle in the nearby brush to get a better look around the area.

"This place is going to be a problem," he mumbled as he avoided the security cameras placed strategically around the perimeter. He wasn't a security expert, but he could tell by the high tech equipment that he wouldn't be gaining entrance. There were a few high trees and surrounding brush that might help him clear the height of the fence, but there was no way he could go in undetected. He would have to wait until they left the property before he could get to his next victim. Richard Daley climbed back in his vehicle to wait them out.

"Yes, he'll do nicely. They won't even be expecting it."

Kate Allenton

CHAPTER 11

Abby didn't think they would ever leave her hospital room. After her release, she now sat in Sam's SUV. Fear settled in her gut. This was no longer a random murderer but a lunatic after the people she cared most about. She clasped her trembling hands together in her lap. She wasn't sure if it was the drugs responsible for her shot nerves or Sam's proximity. Her leg throbbed, and pain radiated from the black-and-blue area, but she couldn't take her eyes off the man behind the wheel.

Sam started the ignition and stared out the window for a brief second before turning his gaze on her. "Let's get you settled and then we'll talk."

She didn't know where they were going, but there wasn't a place in town she couldn't recognize from the landscape alone. She kept her eyes out the window. Darkness had settled in while she'd been in the hospital, and she hoped it wasn't a sign of things to come. She could barely make out the trees lining the road, but she could still sense their location. His cologne was intoxicating, and she absorbed it into her brain. She had a hard time keeping her gaze focused on the passing trees and not on the man in the car that was only an arm's length away. Abby closed her eyes, remembering his caresses from eighteen years ago, and wondered if his hands would still be so smooth, or if the years apart had been hard on him. Eighteen years before they had fumbled through their first time.

She knew that wouldn't be the case now. *Why couldn't he be bald and fat, instead of so yummy?* It just wasn't fair. John deserved a father. She just wasn't sure she could trust him. The secret he had just revealed was a doozy, but her bombshell had the potential to change his life, and Abby didn't know what to expect.

They pulled up to a two-story log cabin on the outskirts of town hidden behind a grove of lush apple trees. She hadn't even known the cabin was here. It was so well hidden from the street. She shifted in her seat to get a better look.

"It's my house," he said as he got out of the car and opened her door. He carried her encased in his steel arms, gentle enough and careful not to hurt her bruise as he made his way to the door.

"Sam, put me down. I can walk."

He eased her down, sliding her body against his when he reached the door. His muscles flexed under her palms, and her breath caught. *God, I still want this man. Geesh already, get your head in the game so you can go home again.*

Sam slid open a panel near the doorframe and started punching numbers. He scooped her up in her strong arms and again carried her inside the house gently placing her on the couch. Abby sighed then frowned. The warmth of his skin touching hers was already fleeting, but his slight touch sent tingles through her traitorous body. Damn it, she still wanted this man. Abby shook her head to clear her thoughts. Those thoughts didn't have a right to be in her head, not with such uncertainty surrounding their future.

"You bought a house here?" She looked up into his eyes, sure that confusion showed on her face. The décor was pleasant enough. The tan couch was comfy, and a stone fireplace graced the wall across from where she sat with her legs propped on the couch. She turned, keeping her leg immobile and scanned the rest of the crème-colored walls, there wasn't a picture in sight. After a few minutes, Sam reentered the room, handing her a steaming cup of coffee, and placed a pillow behind her back. He made her physically comfortable, but emotionally she was a basket case and knew she needed to explain. Sam lit a fire. The warmth from the fireplace touching her skin didn't replace Sam's touch. She couldn't see much from her position. Furniture filled the room, but it was scarce of personal belongings. No knickknacks lying around, there wasn't a woman's touch anywhere to be seen.

Sam rubbed the back of his neck and stayed in front of the fire poking the logs. The only sound heard was the crackling of the embers. "Just because I couldn't be with you, Abby, didn't mean I didn't want to be. I tracked you down after college and the military and bought this place, hoping maybe one day we could find a way to be together."

He turned and walked toward her. She opened her mouth to speak and closed it just as he placed a gentle kiss on her lips. His soft lips grazed hers and were gone before she could pull him into her embrace. He straightened to his full height.

"I need to make some arrangements."

Pulling his phone from his clip, he left her with only her thoughts to keep her company. Abby sipped her coffee and settled into the couch to wait on his return, barely able to keep her eyes open. The events of the day had drained her physically and mentally. She closed her eyes.

****

Sam pushed open one of the swinging doors to the living room for the millionth time to check on his sleeping beauty. Each time he lost his train of thought and the conversation on his cell phone fell silent. He exhaled a breath and eased the swinging door closed.

"Sam, I'm sure she's fine," Stone, his long-time protector and mentor, said again.

"I know. I just can't believe she's here, and I'm worried about her safety. I can't figure out why Daley is here. He must have followed me, and now he knows where she lives. I can't believe I let my guard down. If anything happens to her, Stone..." Sam sat back down at the kitchen table and took another sip of his beer. The liquid did little to douse the worry coursing through his veins. He had to keep reminding himself why he couldn't go back in there, carry her to his bed, and make love to the only woman who'd ever held his heart.

"We'll keep her safe, but you can't keep her under lock and key. You're going to need her help, Sam. She's the best in her field, and could help us catch this guy, and if I had to guess, I think maybe his fixation on you might have transferred to her. You said Daley swerved at the last minute. That's not like the cold-blooded killer we know him to be."

Sam's blood boiled at the thought he'd brought Daley into her life. There was no keeping her out of it now, and he knew it. He would just have to be extra careful and keep his head in the game. "That's why I'm so worried. All of the years I've stayed away from her, trying not to bring this into her life, and what does she do? She gets a job with the damn police and actually does this shit for a living. There's no way in hell I'm ever leaving her again. She stays in way too much danger, damn it." Staying away from her had always been hard. Buying a house in the same town was as close to her as he knew he could get. Now, he was wondering if he shouldn't have gotten closer. Not only was she in a dangerous profession, but he might have learned about his son.

"And now you have a kid. What are you going to do about John?"

Sam knew that question was coming, and he didn't have the slightest idea how to answer. What was he going to do about his son? The son he'd never known he had. "First of all, he's not a kid. He's eighteen. He's the same age I was when I first met Abby. He doesn't trust me and doesn't think I'm going to stick around. On top of all that, he doesn't want anything to do with me. What can I do but wait him out? God knows I have the patience of a saint to have stayed away as long as I have from her, but Stone, I just can't do it anymore."

"Sam, everything is going to be okay. We'll keep them both safe from the lunatic and put him behind bars this time."

"What makes this time any different? He's eluded me for a long time."

"We have Abby on our side, and not only is she one hell of an investigator, but Daley must have taken a fancy to her. We can use that to our advantage."

"Absolutely fucking not. We aren't using her as bait. She's mine now, and I plan to keep it that way." He crushed the picture he had in his hand, one of Richard Daley that he had clipped to the file laying on the counter.

"Relax, Sam. Go put your sleeping beauty to bed and we'll talk again in the morning. In the meantime, I'm going to dig around to see what connection Daley has in Southall."

Sam disconnected the call and balled his fist tight. The urge to pound Daley's head in, overwhelmed him. Red clouded his vision at even the thought of using Abby to catch this freak. Hell no. There was no way in hell, and he'd make sure Stone knew so in the morning when his flight arrived.

CHAPTER 12

Voices drifted to Abby's ears, pulling her from her deep sleep. Sunlight crept through the curtains on the window. A window she didn't recognize. She turned her head, taking in the unfamiliar room where she lay. The enormous bed that looked like it could sleep three comfortably only took up half the room. The rest of it consisted of a couple of strategically placed dressers, one with a mirror, and two closed doors. Abby rolled in the bed and inhaled deeply. Sam's scent hit her, and the memories of the previous day came rushing back to her. *I'm at Sam's.* She sighed. They needed to talk, and there was no time like the present. She flung the covers off and looked down at the clothes covering her body. *Where did these come from?* Abby pulled the shirt away from her body to get a better look. She had on a faded blue concert t-shirt that hung to her knees with only her bra and panties underneath.

She looked around the room for her clothes. They weren't anywhere to be seen. *Damn.* Her face heated at the thought of Sam undressing her. *How did I sleep through that?* She knew her body was in good physical shape, but what she wouldn't have given to be awake and feel his hands on her bare skin. She felt her cheeks redden just from the thought.

Abby cleared her throat, the dryness making it difficult to swallow. She noticed the pitcher of water and aspirin on the bedside table and reached for them. Her leg still throbbed. Her body ached all over, but her headache was pounding. Maybe she had hit her head harder then the doctor thought. The pain wasn't enough to keep her down. She had work to do and a killer to catch, only then would she worry about what the future might hold for them. She threw her head back and downed two of the little white pills, chasing them with a full glass of water. The need to pee hit her instantly. She looked around the massive room, focusing finally on the two closed doors and prayed one of them was the bathroom. What she wouldn't give to take a nice hot shower. It just might help clear her thoughts, so she could focus on the upcoming conversation about John.

She smiled in triumph as she pushed open the first door, and it opened up to a spacious bathroom. Wrought iron fixtures with intricate ornate design hung from the walls. Chiseled granite countertops covered the expansive space. The crème wall covering and beauty of the vast room wasn't what made her heart skip a beat. It was the huge Jacuzzi style tub that made her heart go pitter-patter. The Grecian bathroom should have had a claw-style tub, and the Jacuzzi looked out of place, but it would serve her purpose. Abby hobbled back into the other room to the solid oak dresser in search of something to put on under her large shirt. She wasn't expecting to find any clothes her size but would find something to rig so she didn't feel so exposed. She grabbed a pair of sweatpants from the drawer, raised them to her nose, and inhaled. Sam's smell tickled her nose, and she smiled.

Abby looked up into the mirror at her reflection, and her gaze was caught by what hung on the mirror frame. She pulled the pictures down and stared. She remembered taking those pictures eighteen years ago. She smiled. They'd been at the beach in one of those instant photo booths, making silly faces at the camera.

There were only three, and Abby had a vague memory of there being four. *Maybe he lost one.* She replaced the pictures and pulled the sweatpants over her legs, wincing from the tightness of her aching body, pulled the string tight, and tied it. It would have to do until she could go back to her house and get her clothes, not that she relished the thought of her jeans rubbing against her bruise, but she would figure something out. She ran her hands through her hair to get rid of some of the knots and pulled the door open, making it impossible to avoid hearing the two voices getting louder.

Abby tiptoed up the hall to the open living room where she saw Sam talking to the man she'd once known as his father but now knew to be FBI agent Stone. Steeling her nerves, she entered the room. The conversation came to an abrupt halt.

"What are you doing out of bed?" Sam asked as he stalked over to stand in front of her.

"That's generally what you do when you wake up, although I could use a shower." Abby smiled. His expression cleared from the scowl he wore to a smile of his own as he leaned down and planted his lips on hers. This kiss wasn't like the chaste ones from earlier.

"Abby, I'm not letting you go this time." Sam declared and placed his hands on her hips, pulling her body flush with his. His rigid bulge poked into her belly, making his desire evident. She gasped her surprise and moaned as Sam tilted his head to deepen the kiss. His tongue melding with hers in a sensuous dance, he explored every crevice in her mouth. The tingling from his touch rocked through her body. She wanted more. She wanted everything to do with this man.

The sound of Stone clearing his throat made Sam take a step back, putting some distance between their bodies, but not letting go. He kissed her this time on the cheek and smiled down at her. "Good Morning."

Abby's body was on fire. Desire for the man in front of her assaulted her senses and clouded her judgment. She shook her head and turned toward Agent Stone. "I'm sorry for the interruption."

Stone stepped up to her, his large hand engulfing her fingers. The kiss he placed on her knuckles was quick and sweet. "Don't be ridiculous. It's good to see you again, Abby, and I'm glad you're okay," he said while releasing her hand and turning toward the door. "Sorry I can't stay, but I need to go talk to your captain." He left them staring at the now closed door.

Abby walked to the window to watch the black SUV drive away. *Must be the car of choice for all cops.* She chuckled. *And murderers too.* She shivered at her thought. She turned her face toward Sam's, "What was that about?"

Stroking the stubble of his beard, he regarded her carefully. "Why don't you get a shower first, while I cook you something to eat? Then we'll talk about it."

Abby took two tentative steps into his personal space and placed her palms on the rock hard wall of his chest. "We can't keep putting it off. We need to talk now."

He placed a finger under her chin and lifted her face up to his. This was the man she had loved her entire life. The thought of losing him again made her pull from his light hold. She backed up out of his embrace. Abby needed the distance to think clearly.

"Let's get you cleaned and fed, and then we'll talk." He left her staring at his retreating back. Before he pushed through the swinging doors, he stopped with his hand on the wood and turned to her. The grin on his face and his dimples were almost enough to make her melt on the spot. "Call me if you need any help." He pushed through the doors and was gone.

Abby entered the bedroom and eased down on the bed, resting her head on the soft pillow, thinking about the upcoming conversation. She knew this was a pivotal talk they were about to have. It could change everything. She wasn't going to get anything accomplished lying in bed. She pushed herself up and headed to the bathroom.

Abby pulled a towel from a linen closet and noticed the same bottle of goop that the doctor had put on her bruises and abrasions lying on the counter next to some more bandages. She glanced in the shower and noticed several showerheads overhead and coming down the wall. As much as she wanted to relax in the tub, let the water wash away all of her pain, and enjoy herself, she wasn't going to postpone the inevitable. She eased in the shower instead and washed her body and hair quickly. After dressing and refastening her jewelry, she picked up a brush from the counter and ran it through her hair to get the tangles out. She dressed in Sam's clothes and went in search of her summer sweetheart.

Kate Allenton

CHAPTER 13

Sam sensed Abby's presence in the large kitchen as he gazed out the window. He didn't have to turn around to know that she stood there staring at him. Had she believed him at the hospital? Did she know he was telling the truth? Was it possible the gods would smile down on him and she might still love him even after all these years? He had lived a solitary life, but he was no angel. Other questions ran through his mind before he turned to face her.

The sight of Abby licking her lips had him wanting to drop to his knees to beg the petite beauty to forgive him. Sam stood taller as he walked over to the table and pulled out a chair, gesturing for her to sit down. He hadn't been expecting the chaste kiss she put on his shoulder in passing.

"You feel better?" he asked as he went back to the counter and grabbed the omelets he had made. The toast and fruit already on the tiny table would help her regain her strength.

"Much better, thank you."

Sam sat down to join her. He watched her picking at the omelet, checking for something. Once she seemed satisfied, she took a bite. Her tongue darted out, running across her lips. A look of pure bliss crossed her face, the same look he had only seen once before. She must have definitely approved of his cooking. God, she was beautiful. Sam wanted to grab her and carry her back to his room to get reacquainted with her body that was calling to him, but he held himself back, unsure of the outcome of the conversation they were about to have. He prayed she didn't take this the wrong way. Her safety meant more to him than anything else in the world, even his heart.

Sam took a sip of his coffee, watching her take a few more bites. She placed her fork down and her hands on the table. His hand immediately covered hers. He gave a gentle squeeze. "Abby...I want you off the case. Please go with your sister and John out of town?"

Abby almost spit out the food she was chewing, startled by his request that she leave. After all of these years, and all of the secrets they had just shared, *that* was what he chose to say? *Not bloody likely.* If he thought she'd just leave, he had a thing or two to learn about her.

"No, you need me to help you catch Daley, and besides, you can't make me."

Abby withdrew her hand from his and placed it in her lap. If she was going to keep a straight head, she

couldn't do it while he was touching
her.

"Abby, it'll be safer if you just
leave. I don't know what I would do if
something happened to you because
of me."

Abby held his gaze. He wasn't
getting rid of her this time. No matter
how much he begged or tried to get
her to run. She wasn't leaving.

"Sam, if you think you could get
me to leave and give up on this case,
then I'd have to say you don't know
me at all." Abby rose from the table
and walked out of the room in search
of her purse.

Sam followed. "What are you
doing?"

"I'm looking for my phone so I
can call someone to come get me."
She stopped her search and turned
back to the man who was trying to
run her off.

"Look, I understand there's a
bunch of baggage between us, and I
understand that it may be too much
for you. But, Sam, what you need to
understand about me is that I don't

run from my commitments. I've committed to capturing this lunatic, and I'm damn good at my job. Now that I know he's the reason behind my broken heart and threatens the safety of our son, I'm only pissed off more, and trust me, you haven't seen me pissed off yet. Where's my damn phone?"

"Abby, you're not leaving." Sam stood with his arms crossed over his muscular chest. He ran his hand over his face and through his already tousled hair. He sure was cute when he was trying to show his alpha side. If the situation didn't threaten her family, she might have had to jump him. To bad. It wasn't going to work on her this time. She had too much at stake. This lunatic was going down or she would die trying.

"Like hell you say. Sam, you don't get to decide what I do, and trust me, there are enough males in my life to tell you that you won't win." She smirked because she knew it was the truth.

"Abby, let's sit down and discuss this." He made a gesture toward the couch before sitting down and waited for her to take a seat. "I'm not leaving you, Abby. I just want you to be safe. I've stayed clear of you so he wouldn't find you, and after your accident, I think he's changed his target from me to you. I don't want to lose you."

Abby jumped up from her spot on the couch. "That's great," she said enthusiastically. Her smile widened as she rubbed her hands together. "I need my phone."

"Abby, didn't you hear a word I said? He's after you now, baby."

Abby walked over to Sam and took his hands into hers then she rubbed her thumbs over the outside of his palms. "Sam, I know. This is even better than I thought. Don't you see? Instead of chasing him, we can get him to come to us."

Sam's scowl indicated his displeasure with her plan, but that wasn't going to stop her. She'd find someone else to help her catch this asshole. Her mind was racing. *Maybe Butch will help.*

"Hell no." He pulled his hands from her grasp and balled his fists. "You aren't doing this."

"Suit yourself. This asshole is going down, and I'm sure the captain will see things my way." Abby turned and was now pulling out drawers, looking for her purse. She went to the cordless phone and dialed her cell. She heard it ringing in the bedroom and found her purse lying on the other side of the bed. Abby pulled it out and dialed the only people she knew who would help her.

"Jake, I need your help. Can you please leave John and Emma at your house and station some guards around the place, then come and get me? I've got a plan, and it involves you."

Sam's muscular body was leaning on the doorframe and listened to her call. Abby turned to him. "What's the address here?"

Sam just shook his head. He must have thought she was going to get herself killed. She'd figure it out.

She turned back toward the dresser and sighed. "He won't tell me the address, but we're on the outside of town near the apple trees. Just ask Emma. He has a cabin back off the road."

Abby listened then smiled brightly before she laughed. "I'll see you in fifteen minutes."

"He won't find us out here." Sam's eyes slightly narrowed and held her gaze. His smoldering voice mocked her.

Abby gritted her teeth before she said something she'd regret. She felt the corner of her mouth twitch before she smiled and spoke.

"He already knows where I am." Abby looked down at her watch then held her arm up. "He told me after Emma's kidnapping he didn't ever want to go through that again. He gave one of these to all of us as bridesmaid gifts. He's a genius. It has a tracking device in it." Abby shook her head. "You know that really should piss me off, but it's kinda sweet in a geeky way. Don't you think?"

She was touched that he didn't want to see her get hurt again. He thought he was doing her a favor, saving her from the threat, but honestly he didn't know the woman she had grown up to be.

"Sam, I can do this. I've trained my whole life against people like him. I'm smart and stronger than you're giving me credit for. I'm not jumping into this half-cocked. I'm going to plan first before I ever make my first move." Abby slid up to him and threw her arms around his big body. If something did happen to her, she wouldn't take any regrets to the grave.

Slowly his hands encircled her in his embrace. She laid her cheek against his wide chest and felt like she was home. She needed this man like she needed her next breath. His palms rubbed slow circles on her back, and she looked up into his smoldering blue eyes. He raised a hand to her face. His skillful fingers tenderly traced her lips before he leaned down and kissed her. Sam ran his tongue over the seam of her lips demanding entrance, and she obliged, opening up for his assault. She had just slid her hands up to his neck and was pulling him down to deepen the kiss when the buzz from the doorbell interrupted their embrace.

Abby pulled out of his arms and placed her hands on her hips. She knew the man outside wasn't leaving here without her. It was just a matter of whether or not Sam was coming with her. "Pack a bag, Bennett, and grab your files. You're coming with me," Abby demanded and walked out of the room to open the door for Jake.

Jake's hand was perched in the air, as if he was about to knock again when she pulled the door open and invited him in. Jake picked her up and squeezed, making her body ache's hurt worse, she tried to squirm out of his embrace. "That hurt." She hit him on the arm.

"Why didn't you tell me about this before today?" Abby lifted her arm and shook her watch in front of his face.

His expression cleared, and his grin faded. "After Emma was kidnapped, I'm surprised you even have to ask."

Abby threw her arms around her brother-in-law. "I'm not mad; you're a genius. I just wish you would have told me how cool it is." She took the watch off and turned it over before she looked up at him and asked, "Where's the tracker?"

She knew how tech savvy he was. His whole house was consumed with gadgets and stuff that he had constructed himself. His security system was better than the one at Ft. Knox, and that was what she was counting on.

Jake didn't point to where she thought he'd put it in the battery compartment. He pointed to the band. I had it woven into the band. I knew you girls wouldn't ever get rid of the three-carat diamonds in those bands. Besides, when the battery dies, I didn't want to chance the watchmaker finding it when he replaced the battery."

Abby put her hands on her hips. "Does Emma know?"

Jake threw his hands up in the air. "Of course she does. Whose idea do you think it was to include the diamonds? We even gave one to John. Don't worry. We won't impose on your privacy. It's just for emergencies."

CHAPTER 14

Abby stood on her tiptoes, squeezed his neck, and whispered, "thank you," in his ear.

Sam cleared his throat, and Jake moved to place Abby behind his back, as if protecting her from the big bad wolf. Sam had his duffle bag over his shoulder, and a box of files in his arms. He looked ready to go.

Abby pushed Jake out of the way and touched his arm. "It's okay; he's coming with us. He just doesn't know what I'm capable of, and he's scared for me." She smiled sweetly at her brother-in-law. It was really kind of sweet the way the men in her life wanted to protect her and thought she was crazy for not running scared like a schoolgirl.

Jake looked from her to Sam and settled his gaze on her. "Uh, Abby, where are we going?"

"We're going to your house, but Sam is going to be taking me. I need you to call Butch and gather the troops before you send Emma and John to the beach house to keep them safe. Did you make those changes to the security at the beach house?"

"Abby, you know me better than that."

"I know, but you know me too. I have to know they're going to be safe and away from what I have planned."

Sam dropped his box to the floor and walked over to Abby, placing his arm around her shoulder before he spoke to Jake. "Can't you talk her out of this?"

Jake looked at Abby, cocked his head to the side, and raised an eyebrow. "Is he serious?"

"It's okay Jake; he still has a lot to learn about me. We'll fill him in when we get there."

The ride to Emma and Jake's house didn't take long. Sam was silent during the ride. Abby wished there was a way to alleviate his fear for her safety. She knew she was just going to have to prove it. Emma and John were waiting on the porch with Butch by their side. They all had their arms crossed over their chests. Abby's lips tilted up. She had some explaining to do.

Abby looked at Sam and squeezed his hand. "I'm sorry Sam, I didn't even think that this might be hard for you, you don't have to stay. It's okay." Sam placed his palm on her cheek, leaned in, and brushed his soft lips against hers. "We're in this together, baby. Besides, he's going to have to get used to me eventually. I'm not going anywhere, not even when this is over. Abby, the only reason I stayed away was because of Daley. Now that he's here, there's no reason for me to leave. I've waited for so long to be with you, and now it's possible."

Abby's heart expanded. She felt another brick around her heart crumble and leaned into his palm before lifting her head and placing a kiss to his now empty palm. She would find a way to work this out for them if it was the last thing she did. They all deserved a chance. Abby pulled the handle and stepped out of the car. She waited at the front of the SUV for Sam. She wasn't going to leave him behind, not now that her heart was in it. He walked to her side, and she took his hand and walked by his side toward her waiting family.

"What the hell is he doing here?" John asked as he walked toward them and stood in front of his father.

"He's here because of us, John. There's been a change of plans, and I wanted to talk to you before you leave with Aunt Emma."

John looked from Abby to Sam and back before turning to stomp back into the house. Abby had known this would be hard on him, but there were things that needed to be said before he left.

Emma walked over and hugged her. Her sister must have seen distress on her face at her son's retreat. "Everything's going to be fine, little sister. We'll work this out." Emma placed her arm around her shoulder and walked with her toward the house.

Butch touched her arm. "Are you sure about this?"

His look was sincere. Was he worried about her safety or her heart? She didn't know which, but she was just glad he was on her side either way. "I'm sure." She whispered and looked back at Sam, who let out a sigh as he walked behind her.

They walked into her sister's favorite place in the house, the library. It was where Emma had revealed her secret that she loved Jake to her sisters. It had been a big step in Emma's life, and it was a calming place. A fire was set in the stone fireplace. An open book sat flipped upside down on the table as a marker, holding a page. The desk at the end of the room was spotless like the last time. The lights were slightly dimmed. John stood there in front of the shadows, watching the flames dance with his back to them.

Emma grabbed Jake's and Butch's arms and pulled them from the room. "We're going to start dinner while we wait on Briggs. Whenever you're ready, we'll be in the kitchen." Emma clicked the door closed for privacy.

Abby walked up to her son and placed her hand on his arm. "Please sit with me so we can talk about all of this."

He pulled his arm away from her, and her gaze went down to the floor. He was her baby, and he was pushing her away. How was she going to break through his hard exterior? He needed her now more than ever, and she needed to make him see things her way. Abby walked to the couch and took a seat across from Sam. A safe distance so her son wouldn't feel so alienated. John came, sat down beside her, and grabbed her hand.

"He's just going to hurt you again."

"John, let him explain, and then you can judge when you have all the facts. If I've taught you anything growing up, it was to listen to all of the facts." Abby gently squeezed his hand.

"You're right, Mom. Your life is based on facts. I'll hear him out."

Abby wanted to jump for joy at this small victory but knew better. She let out a breath she didn't realize she'd been holding, and finally thought for the first time since she'd been eighteen, everything might actually work out.

Sam and Abby proceeded to tell John everything, from their first meeting to his conception, and why Sam had stayed away. They covered his changed identity, his stint in the military, then college, and explained Richard Daley's involvement and how he tried to keep her safe. Abby knew her mouth hung open when Sam turned to her and said he loved her. A tear trickled down her face. Richard Daley had robbed her of so much lost time.

John looked at Abby. His face, so much like his father's, was blank, not even betraying a hint of what he was thinking.

"Mom did you tell him everything about us, including what only our family knows?" John tilted his head to the side, and he raised his eyebrow

It was obvious her answer would affect the outcome, and she wanted to kick herself for not thinking about it first. There had been times when she could have told him, and maybe her heart was still too fragile, thinking he might leave her. Because of her insecurities from his return, she had held off telling him about their abilities. Hell, he was FBI. If things didn't work out, there was a chance, if he knew, their lives could change for the worse.

"Not yet." Abby's gaze went to Sam's. Regret had made her heart fall to her stomach.

"Then he's the one missing all of the facts, and the jury's still out. This is a lot to take in."

John left them alone in the room and for the second time in her life, Abby was at a loss, unsure how to make everything okay for John. Sam rose and went to her side, pulling her up from the couch and into his embrace. His arms circled around her. Abby laid her face on his stone chest and felt the tears slide down her face. Keeping the truth about their abilities might have done more harm than good. She'd known this was going to be hard, but she hadn't expected it to break her heart. Resigned there was nothing she could do about it, she swiped her hands across her face. She tilted her head up and looked up into his eyes. Her hand rose to his face. "Sam, I can't force him to accept this, he's lived his whole life thinking that you lied and abandoned us. I'm so sorry. "

He turned to kiss her palm. "Me too, baby. What did he mean that I didn't have all the facts?"

"I still have a few things to tell you about my family, but it can wait for now."

They walked hand in hand to the kitchen, where they found everyone working in tandem to get an impromptu dinner prepared. Briggs had made it, but John was nowhere to be seen. Emma squeezed her arm as she passed.

"Are you okay?"

Abby shook her head, afraid that if she tried to speak her voice would break.

"I'll go check on him, Abby. He's just worried about you. I'm sure he just needs some space and to let this all soak in. Besides, he can fill me in." She winked and left the room. Abby stared at the occupants of the kitchen. All eyes were focused on her, and their questioning stare showed they didn't understand her choice, but it wasn't theirs to make. She threw her shoulders back, stood taller, and took command of their little group. She wouldn't be changing her mind about the plan she'd formed in her head or the man by her side. Her happiness depended on it.

"Something smells good." Abby smiled and walked to the coffee pot. "You all know Sam. Sam, this is everyone; this is my family. Well, all but Claire is here," she teased, Pouring two cups of coffee, she returned to his side, handing him a cup of the steaming brew. Abby felt the brush of his arm as he placed his arm around her shoulder. The weight should have been heavy, but it wasn't. The feel was comforting. He kissed the top of her head before everyone turned back to preparing their meal. Butch was the first to walk over to them and offer his hand. Sam took it. The gesture was more than she thought he would get. Butch let go of his hand, opened his stance, and crossed his arms over his chest. His jaw twitched before he said, "You hurt her, and you're dead."

The testosterone that filled the room rolled in waves toward her like an unforeseen force. Abby just shook her head. He wouldn't be the last to threaten Sam. "Butch, Sam is in this as much as I am, we're going to catch this guy, and then work out the rest." Abby gestured to everyone in the room, their eyes now riveted on the two. "Hell, look what he's having to deal with. If this were reversed, would any of you want me walking into a room filled with animosity and threats?"

Abby pulled Sam to the table and took a seat as the food was being put down. Conversations erupted around them, almost like at their family dinners. There was still a dark cloud hanging over her head, and she needed to come clean about her plan she had concocted to use herself as bait, but it could wait. These men were grumpy when they didn't eat. She needed them well fed if she was going to persuade them to help with her quest. She crossed her fingers and said a silent prayer. Dinner went off without a hitch with no punches thrown and no insults tossed in Sam's direction. Well, no more than the usual banter between the men sitting around her, and that was the best she could hope for. John had decided to join them, quiet as he was. He took the seat to her left.

Once everyone was finished eating and the dishes cleared, Abby stood and cleared her throat. She shoved her hands in the pockets of the jeans she'd borrowed from Emma, to hide the slight tremor. She knew what needed to be done. Everyone turned toward her. Most held a skeptical look, they were accustomed to her crazy ideas, but they waited patiently.

"There's been a recent development in my current case. Most of you know I'm after a killer, well his name is Richard Daley." Sam stood behind her and placed his hands on her shoulders. His big body towered over her. She could feel his muscles pressed against her back. A quiver ran through her. He must have sensed she needed the support, when trying to convince her family, why she should be running head on into a danger. They weren't going to like why it had turned personal, but that wouldn't change the fact that it had. Abby told them the whole story of how Richard Daley had ruined her life eighteen years ago. "Sam tells me Daley seems to have changed his MO when he didn't kill me, and it has left most of the FBI agents on the case scrambling to figure out why. Sam and his mentor seem to think..." Abby leaned her head back and smiled at Sam. "He didn't kill me for a reason. Agent Stone seems to think that now he's going to be after me. If nothing else, then to get at Sam. This is all just a game to Daley, and the last one standing wins."

Butch jumped to his feet, and his nostrils flared. "We'll kill him. We'll track the bastard down, and we'll kill him. He won't touch you, Abby." All of her family stood and started pulling their guns out, checking their rounds as they broke in conversation trying to devise a plan to keep her safe.

Abby stomped her foot before she yelled. "Sit back down. I'm not finished." Startled, they each froze, their conversations stopped in their tasks. "Please, sit down." Her request came out as a whisper, and unbelievably, they complied.

"Actually, this is a good thing," Abby interjected.

Butch rose again, about to intercede until Abby gave him a pleading look and he sat back down. "This means that we don't have to chase him. He'll come to me."

"Absolutely not, we aren't going to risk your life." Jake interjected from his seat at the table. "Your sisters would string me up if anything happened to you. Abby, you've got to be reasonable." Emma rubbed his arm.

"Just hear her out." Emma gave her a weak smile.

"Jake, you're responsible for getting Emma, Claire, and John out of here. Have Briggs take them to the beach house. Unfortunately, I need you to stay here."

Her sister slid her chair back, scraping it against the wood floors, and stood to her regal height. Abby had seen that look on her face before. Her eyes shooting daggers, Emma obviously disagreed with her plan. She placed her hands on her hips and vehemently shook her head from side to side. "I don't think so."

"Emma please, think about the baby. I need to know that you, Claire, and John are safe. I won't be able to keep my head in the game if I have to worry about all of you.

For once Jake agreed and pulled Emma into his lap as he buried his face in her hair. He placed a kiss before whispering something in her ear, a secret meant only for her.

Butch interrupted their embrace. The scowl on his face meant Abby hadn't convinced him and wasn't done trying to get everyone on board. "You…" He pointed his finger at Sam. "You agreed with this plan?" he asked, his tone accusing.

"Hell no, I don't agree with her plan. I wish I could lock her up in my house and keep her safe, but you know her better than I do. I'd wager that she'd probably find a way to escape and never forgive me."

Truer words had never been spoken; there was no way she was sitting by when this concerned Sam. Abby was in charge of her own destiny. Her fate rested on her own shoulders now. Sam was back in her life, and she would fight tooth and nail until the end to keep her family together. Losing wasn't an option she could live with.

Abby pulled in a breath and released it slowly. "Butch, I love you, but I'm doing this with or without your help. You can all just get on board, or I'll figure this out on my own. This man has taken too much from me for me to just sit by and hope someone else comes up with a better plan."

Briggs, normally quiet, chimed in. "My money is on the princess. Abby, if you need my help, consider it done."

Abby's smile grew bigger as she took in the silent giant's words. He wasn't someone who spoke often, he liked to calculate and evaluate every more before he made them. His approval spoke volumes. "Finally," she said with sigh. "Thanks, Briggs."

Briggs' words stunned the rest of them into silence. He gave his help willingly, which is more than she could say for the rest. He believed in her.

Butch gazed into her eyes. His silent plea for her safety went unanswered. He dropped his gaze to the table and mumbled. "What's your plan?"

She wanted to jump up and down like a five-year-old given a piece of candy, clapping her hands in triumph, but she refrained. "I'm the bait. We can work out the details tomorrow because I'm dead tired." Her gaze flew to Emma's. "Which room can we stay in?"

CHAPTER 15

Exhausted, Abby laid her head down on the soft pillow. Darkness consumed her before Sam even emerged from the shower. Abby blinked and stretched. Her hand lightly poked the body in bed with her. *I slept with Sam.* Sam was lying on his stomach with his face turned from her. He hadn't even flinched from her poke. *The poor guy must be really tired.* Abby silently threw her legs off the side of the bed and slid out of the comfort of the covers. There was no time like the present to get started on the files about Daley.

After a shower and changing into some of the clothes her sister had left her, she padded down the stairs toward the smell of coffee. The sight of John sitting at the table in the early morning hours startled her. He was digging through Sam's box of files. *When did he get those?* She must have been more tired than she thought. John walked over to the coffee pot, came back with a steaming mug, and handed it to her. It had been a long week, and Abby needed it to kick-start her brain into functioning.

"Well, I guess we need to figure this out. I'm not going to lie and tell you that I like your plan to be used as bait. But I trust that you know what you're doing and besides you have the guys to help you catch this psycho. So I thought I'd help."

John pulled another file out of the box and opened it. He wasn't an investigator, but a son on a mission trying to help his mom. Abby kissed his cheek.

"I love you, John," she whispered in his ear. She was so proud of the man he'd become. She couldn't have hoped for better. Abby sat down and sipped her coffee while watching her son look through the files. Her heart swelled with pride. She should have known he would be in this with her. The goofy grin she must be wearing said it all.

John handed her a file. "Why don't you dig in? The better we know this guy, the more likely we can figure out his next move."

"When did you get so smart?" Abby asked. She could feel her heart expanding as gratitude and love overwhelmed her.

"I learned it from you. It must be in our DNA." John looked up at her and smiled.

Abby took the file, thinking, *I'm so blessed.* She had just started her third file when everyone else began to trickle in, starting breakfast and asking questions she'd tuned out. A picture from the file had her

Kate Allenton

engrossed. There was something about it, but she couldn't put her finger on it. She didn't even notice when Sam had came into the kitchen until he leaned down and placed a kiss on the top of her wet hair. "That's his first victim, the murder I witnessed."

Abby pulled her gaze from the woman in the picture to his face then looked back at the picture in a new light. "There's something about this picture..."

Emma walked into the room. "Momma Mae said be sure to check out the details." A hush fell over the room, and Emma stopped. "What?" Emma shrugged her shoulders. "You all know she's vague." Emma continued walking toward her waiting husband by the coffee pot.

Sam leaned over and whispered, "Who's Momma Mae?"

She was so engrossed in the picture, she didn't think before she said, "A ghost that only Emma and Jake can see." Abby's hand flew to her mouth as she looked up expectantly at her sister. She hadn't meant to give away one of their family secrets.

"It's okay, Abby. Momma Mae likes him." Emma pointed with her mug toward Sam.

Sam's brows drew together, and his lips turned down in a frown. "A ghost?"

"Yeah, it's a long story. I'll fill you in on the details later. There's a lot we still need to talk about." Abby glanced back down at the picture, trying to take in every small detail, she studied every square inch of the photo. She whispered, "Details, details, details." She tapped her finger to her chin. You could almost see the light turn on. Her eyes widened, and she jumped from her chair, barely missing knocking her coffee over on the table.

"I've got it. I've seen that locket before."

Emma walked over to her and took the picture out of her hand. "Let me see." Emma narrowed her eyes and her brow scrunched together. "It looks just like the same one Mrs. A had on yesterday." She handed her back the picture and went to snuggle on Jake's lap. Emma looked up at her, "What would she be doing with a dead woman's locket?"

"I'm not sure, but it's worth a shot to give her a call. Maybe she knows something."

Jake kissed his wife and repositioned her in the chair he abandoned. He pulled out his cell, dialed a number and hit the speaker button. One ring, then two before the little old lady's voice on the other end filled the room. "Hello."

"Mrs. A, it's Jake, and I need your help."

"Oh hi, dear. How is Emma feeling? Any morning sickness yet?"

Jake glanced to Emma, and she shrugged. No one knew how the old lady knew so much, but they had more pressing questions for her.

"Uh, no, not yet. Mrs. A, Listen, Abby mentioned that she liked a new locket you were wearing. Can you tell me where you got it? I'd like to see about getting Emma one for when the baby comes."

"Oh dear, I don't know where he got it. One of my tenants gave it to me, the same one that I was trying to set Abby up with."

All the men in the room turned their gaze on Abby "What, I said no," she whispered.

"Mrs. A, can you give me his address, and I'll stop by and ask him which store he bought it from. I would really appreciate it.

"Sure dear, he's renting the lake cabin. The address is 115 Lake Drive. Mr. Smith just came to see me today. He was very interested when I mention he needed to meet Abby."

"Mrs. A, will you call me if you see him again?" Jake took the phone off speaker and placed it to his ear, and after a few more quick words, he disconnected the call.

Jake pulled a map from his cabinet and spread it out on the table as Abby moved in closer to view it herself.

"Here it is," Abby said, and pointed at a location on the map. She reached for her ankle holster to pull her gun and realized it wasn't there. She hadn't worn it since leaving the hospital.

Emma walked over to a drawer in the kitchen and pulled one out. She walked back over to Abby and handed it to her. "Here use mine." She smiled down on her sister.

"Thanks Em."

The room had turned silent. She could hear her own breathing. She looked up. "What? I'm not going to run off half-cocked. Give me some credit."

Abby called Mike and informed him of the latest breakthrough. "Mike's going to meet us there."

Everyone but Emma, John, and Briggs piled in the SUVs to head to the lake. The passing scenery did little to settle her nerves. It was déjà vu. They had been down this road before when Ben had kidnapped Emma.

Sam placed his hand in hers and lifted it to his mouth, placing a gentle kiss to her palm. "Abby, I need you to be careful. He wants you. He doesn't care about any of us. If things go bad, I want you to run."

"Sam, I'm not going to run, and you're wrong about one thing. He doesn't want me, he wants to use me to get to you. I'm going to catch this asshole so we can move on with our lives. If we don't, we'll constantly be looking over our shoulders, and I can't live like that." She turned her hand in his and kissed his palm in return.

He pulled his hand from hers and placed it back on the steering wheel. His white from the pressure. Sam took a few deep breaths before he glanced at her. "Your job isn't worth dying over. If you won't be careful for me, then do it for John."

Abby knew he was right. She turned once again toward the window, watching as they passed the tree line, and realized they were getting closer. The afternoon sun beat through the windows on her face. It would have been a peaceful beautiful day if they didn't have a date to meet a lunatic. She'd just found Sam—well, technically, he'd found her—but she wasn't giving up on him yet. "Fine."

They pulled in behind the other SUVs and got out. She couldn't see the cabin through the trees, but she knew it was there. They made their plan, took up positions, and approached the house. Mike had been instrumental when Jake moved his business into town, making sure they had the right permits in their business to carry their guns. The whole force was aware of the bodyguards' capabilities. No one would be startled to see that they were all armed and were converging on a house. Weapons drawn, they inched closer, keeping low to be out of sight in case he was home. The closer they got to the log cabin the quieter it became. No birds sang; no crickets chirped. She heard just the sound of her own breathing as the adrenaline flowed through her veins. They squatted behind the trees and brush, just outside the clearing. The clearing was empty. There was no sight of the silver SUV she had expected to see.

From his spot on the side of the house, Mike gave a hand signal for everyone to stop. He inched closer to the window and peered through. He inched his way around to the back, and then within minutes, he walked to the front and peeked inside another window. He waved them all forward; the coast was clear.

Abby stopped everyone from entering the cabin. If Richard wasn't in there then time was on their side, and they were going to handle this the correct way. She wasn't about to have her evidence thrown out of court on a technicality, so Abby did the one thing that would get her the desired results. She called in another favor. Within twenty minutes of the call, after they all anxiously waited, Ted showed up with the signed search warrant in his hands. Within minutes, Sam kicked down the door, and Abby's mouth dropped open in shock. Plastered around the walls were pictures of her, Sam, John, and her family. He had gotten the drop on

them. They were all oblivious they'd
let him get that close.

A shiver ran down her spine. She
rubbed her arms and spun on her
heel toward Jake. "Call and check on
Emma and John. He's got pictures of
your house." Jake snatched the
phone from the clip and walked
outside, punching numbers. His face
was a shade of red she hadn't seen
before. His nostrils flared, as he held
the phone to his ear. He was pissed,
and she couldn't blame him.

Bile rose from her stomach
toward her throat. Her hand went to
cover her mouth as she walked
around taking in all of the photos
plastered on the walls. Pictures of
her family lay strewn everywhere.
She walked on shaky legs toward the
desk against the wall. A knife lay on
one of the pictures of Sam. The
picture next to it was one of her
leaving Emma's café the day she was
going to meet Sam, the same day
Daley had almost killed her. A red
heart circled her face, his intent was
clear now. Her suspicions hadn't

been right. This asshole wanted her, and now she wanted him to. She could think of a million ways she'd been trained to kill the bastard, and if she was lucky, she might just get to use every one of them.

Abby turned to Mike. "Call it in. I need my team here to start collecting and sorting through the evidence. This fucker is mine."

Mike punched in some numbers as he walked outside with Butch on his heels.

Sam hugged her from behind and placed a kiss on her neck. "I promise, he won't touch you." Abby turned into his embrace and hugged him back, leaning into his arms as they formed a steel band around her body.

She was just thankful her family was still safe and now they knew what to expect. He could have grabbed them at anytime, and they wouldn't have ever seen it coming. She would've had to been lost in her own problems not to notice the dangers lurking nearby. *Well, not anymore, asshole.*

The afternoon passed as the investigative team worked tirelessly on the cabin. They logged photos, dusted for fingerprints, and catalogued stacks of papers and other miscellaneous items they seized. Instead of high-fiving her for making the score, they each gave her a grim smile and nodded as they left. They understood what this meant for her, just like she did. She was in for a long, bumpy ride with no end in sight. Mike strategically placed men on surveillance around the house, and a few followed them all back to Jake's, stationing themselves around the perimeter. Her day had gone down hill when Daley hadn't been home for the take down.

John, Emma, and Briggs again greeted them at the door. John advanced on her, squeezing her tight in a bone-crushing hug. "Jake told us what you found. I'm so sorry, Mom."

John kissed the top of her head, placed her back on her feet, and looked at his father. "I've never asked

you for anything in my life, old man."
John looked down at his feet before
looking back at Sam's eyes. "Promise
me you'll keep her safe from this
bastard. I don't know what I'd do
without her."

As touching as the moment was,
Abby just couldn't stop herself. She
punched her son in the arm. "Snap
out of it. Nothing is going to happen
to me." Then she left them, walking
into the house and up to the room
they'd occupied the night before.
Thoughts swirled in her head, never
stopping on just one thing—Richard
Daley, the cabin, and his involvement
in keeping Sam away. Abby clenched
her fists tight. The more she thought
about everything the more pissed she
got.

Abby wanted a shower. She felt
vulnerable and victimized by what
they had found at the cabin, and she
just wanted to wash away those
feelings. They weren't going to help
her. She needed a clear head, one
that would anticipate Daley's next
move.

Abby stripped on her way to the bathroom, started the water, and climbed in. Water sluiced down her body, washing away the dirt and events from the day. The muscles in her shoulders relaxed. She hadn't realized she'd been so tense. She stood under the shower until she heard the bathroom door shut. Abby didn't want to talk to anyone, not right now. She just wanted to forget so she stood under the hot water and planned to ignore whoever had entered the bathroom. She thought it might be Emma invading her space until the curtain pulled back and Sam stepped in to the small tub.

Sam's tanned muscular chest was at her eye level. The tight chest begged for her to run her fingers over it, tracing his six-pack abs. Abby knew her face was red, but she didn't care. Her gaze ran down the length of his body. His erection protruded out from his body, and her hands itched to feel and stroke his silky length. For that reason, she kept her hands to her sides, even though her gaze traveled down his length taking in every inch of the man. The muscles in his toned biceps flexed as he moved to step closer to her. Abby leaned her head back and looked into the eyes of the only man she had ever truly loved.

"Turn around, Abby," he commanded in a husky voice, and her body immediately obeyed. She turned around so her back was to him, the water spraying on her chest. She heard a pop, and then his fingers were in her hair, massaging shampoo into the length of her hair. Abby sighed. It felt so good; no man had ever washed her hair. He had her step under the warming spray and rinse. She wanted his hands on more places than her hair. She needed his touch all over her body. She wanted to fall to her knees and take him into her mouth but held back from all the desires running through her mind.

Sam repeated the process with the conditioner. He took a bar of soap and lathered it in his hands, covering them in suds before she felt them on her skin. His touch left a trail that felt like fire over her body as he inched his way around her midsection with her back pressed against his hard chest. Evidence of his desire nestled between her cheeks. She felt her cream leak and pool around the place she most desperately wanted him to touch. She hadn't felt like this in years, so alive and responsive to his every touch. His palms inched up her chest and encircled her breast. He gave a gentle squeeze as he lifted their weight in his palms. She felt his erection thicken against her. He wanted her as much as she wanted him. *What would he do if I just turned around? Would he take me against the wall?* The thought thrilled her, and her body responded in kind.

Abby was pulled from her thoughts when Sam increased the circle around her areolas sending more cream to her thighs. He pinched and pulled the extended nubs. Abby's head fell back against Sam's hard chest. The pleasure-pain of his hands built her desire, centering low in her belly. She wondered if he would send her sailing over the top with just his hands caressing her body and nothing else. Abby reached back and grabbed the outside of his thighs, trying to wedge her hands between their touching bodies. She wanted to run her hands over his body and give him back some of the pleasure coursing through her.

"Uh, uh, if you touch me now, I'll explode. Keep your hands right where they are, Abby."

Sam leaned down and kissed her neck, sucking at the water left behind. His tongue traced a path from her collarbone to her ear while his hand inched lower down her body. He whispered, "You're so beautiful."

"I need more," she whispered with desperate need as his hands traveled through her silk curls down to her core. He ran a finger from the back of her slit to the front, pushing in one of his long fingers as his thumb circled her swollen bundle of nerves.

"Oh god." The pleasure was so exquisite. She could feel herself climbing toward her release with every stroke. Her limbs threatened to give out as she concentrated on the pure bliss his hands had on her body. He thrust two more fingers into her and increased his speed.

"You're so tight, baby. I can't wait to be inside of you and feel you fisting my cock."

She thought she might fall to her knees. Sam's other hand bound her waist, forcefully holding her tight against his thick chest. The triple assault of his dirty talk, his mouth suckling her neck, and his fingers delving deeper in and out of her channel were enough to send her over the top. She felt the orgasm building to a crest, unable to hold back anymore, tremors racked her body as she came, screaming his name. Her body shook in the aftermath as Sam held her tight through her release. He turned her body toward his and raised his fingers to his lips. His eyes closed as he sucked his fingers clean.

Abby didn't know how she was even standing. Her pent-up stress and energy washed down the drain with the evidence of her desire.

Sam reached down, turned off the water, and gathered her in a fluffy white towel. He dried her off before carrying her to the bed. He placed her in the middle on the silk sheets and climbed in beside her. Abby turned her head towards him, touched his neck, and pulled him down, crushing his mouth to her waiting lips. She opened her mouth wanting all of him. Tingles raced through her body when his hand cupped her breast and gave a gentle squeeze. Abby arched her chest into his hand wanting more of the exquisite feel. His tongue tangled with hers before he left her mouth and lowered, kissing a path to her breast. His tongue circled her dusty pink nipple while his hand fondled her other one. He gave a slight nip with his teeth before placing his mouth on the neglected twin.

Abby fisted her hands in his hair and pulled him closer to her body as she arched up. Abby knew she should stop him, but her body begged for more. This was what she'd been missing for all of those years. Sam pulled back from her embrace when she stiffened under his hands.

"What's wrong, Abby?"

Abby felt her cheeks redden, but she needed to stop him before it was too late. "We need a condom."

She leaned over to the bedside table where she knew Emma had a stash. Her sister kept them in all of the rooms. She pulled one from the box and ripped the wrapper with her teeth.

"I'm not going anywhere, baby."

She took his silky shaft into her hands and rolled it down before leaning up to place tiny kisses on his chest. "I know."

Sam's crushing kiss had her pressed hard against the pillow as his hand traveled over the dips in her stomach and found her mound. His fingertip ran over her wet folds.

"So wet, so sexy." He pushed his finger in without warning, eliciting a gasp from her lips. Her soreness wouldn't stop her from making love to him. "You're not ready yet. Let me play." He inched down, settling his body between her thighs. Abby's legs fell open to give him more room. His tongue darted out and licked from the bottom of her slit to the top while his finger moved in and out of her. She could feel him coaxing her cream from her body. He removed his finger, licking it as he stared down at her glistening heat.

"Finally, all mine," Abby thought she heard him say, but she couldn't coax a word past her lips when his tongue shoved in deep.

"Oh yes," she whispered.

His thumb circled her clit. He replaced his tongue with his fingers and moved his mouth where his thumb had left. He toyed with the tiny bud against his tongue. He pushed two fingers into her core, scissoring them to stretch her walls.

Just when she didn't think she could handle any more, Sam stopped his ministrations and slid up her body. His shaft poked at her entrance. Sam leaned down and took her mouth in a tender kiss. He lifted up from her and watched her eyes as he slowly inched into her. Wanting more, she arched her back, lifting her pelvis up to him. He waited for her to acclimate to the feel of his thick shaft in her, stretching her.

He slid in to the hilt. Abby released a breath when she grew accustomed to his large size.

"I'm not going to last, baby." He leaned down and breathed into her ear. "You're fisting me like a glove."

Sam slowly pulled out and thrust back in for more. Abby lifted her legs and wrapped them around his waist. She pushed her heels into him, begging for more and urging him on.

"Take me, Sam. Make me yours."

His powerful thrusts quickened as she lifted her body up, meeting him stroke for stroke. He licked his finger, reached down between her thighs, and found the little bundle of nerves he was searching for. He circled her clit, driving her higher, and pressed down hard. She came, screaming his name.

She felt her walls tightened around his shaft. He rammed home one more time, shooting his seed into the rubber barrier she wished wasn't there. She wanted this man. No, she needed this man, more than she needed to breathe.

He collapsed down beside her, pulling her into his arms, right where she knew she belonged. A sense of peace overcame her. Their labored breathing began to slow to normal. He leaned down and pressed his lips tight to hers. It would have melted her if her body weren't already limp.

"I love you, Abby."

"I love you too, Sam."

A grumble came from Abby's stomach during her tender declaration, and she giggled.

Sam pushed himself off the bed and held his hand out to her. "Let's get you showered and fed." He pulled her to the bathroom for another shower that she hoped would turn out the same way.

CHAPTER 16

Abby and Sam descended the staircase, holding hands. Their late afternoon romp had brought them closer than she could have imagined. Abby giggled as Sam whispered sweet nothings into her ear and hit her on the ass as he pushed through the kitchen. She almost tripped, reinforcing the need for her to return to her house for another change of clothes. Though she rolled them up, all of Emma's pants were about a mile too long. Sam followed behind Abby into the kitchen. She inhaled, and the aroma of tomatoes, oregano, and garlic drifted to her nose, making her mouth water. Emma was making her all-time favorite dish. She was bent over the chef stove, pulling out the first of three pans of homemade lasagna when Abby approached. "Let me get those for you. You go sit down and prop up your feet." Abby tried to shoo Emma out of the way while reaching for the oven mitts.

"Oh no you don't. You'd sneak off with a whole pan if I'd let you." Emma grabbed the mitts back and went about pulling the remaining pans from the oven. After that, she grabbed the salad items from the fridge. She handed a knife to Abby with the cucumbers. "Make yourself useful and chop these."

Abby sat at the bar with a cutting board while her sister prepared the rest of the salad. Abby looked over her shoulder. The men were engrossed in their own conversations, now including Sam. Her lips curved in a smile.

Emma leaned over and whispered, "I know that look. You did the dirty with the hunky FBI agent, didn't you?" Emma was acting like a teen, trying to get her to spill the dirty little details of her escapades.

Abby felt the blood drain from her face. "Oh my god, how do you know? Please don't tell me you heard us." She lifted the knife and pointed it accusingly at her sister.

"No, I didn't hear you. I've just never seen you this relaxed, especially with a killer on the loose."

Abby's head fell forward. How could she have been so stupid? Her mind should have been thinking of ways to find the creep, not immersed in pleasure. She wanted to bang her head on the counter.

Emma walked around the counter and placed her hand on her shoulders. "It's okay, Abby. Maybe you just needed to get some of it out of your system so you could concentrate on other things besides his hot body."

Abby felt her face flush.

The rest of the evening went without another word spoken about whatever noises were coming out of their bedroom, and she tuned back into her family.

"When are you leaving for the beach house?" she asked Briggs, knowing that he was the logical choice for protecting Emma and John.

"In the morning when Claire gets back in town. She had to go accept an award for one of her charities."

Concern had her mind spinning. Mike must have noticed the look. "Don't worry, Jake sent Jacobs with her." The tension in her shoulders evaporated. Jake wouldn't let anything happen to any of them. She continued eating her dinner without engaging in more conversations. Sam's fingers, making circles on her thigh, kept making her lose her train of thought. All cohesive words vanished from her mind as she replayed their lovemaking over again in her head. Sam gave a light pinch to her leg, and she looked up into his face. "Ow."

"Jake's talking to you, baby. What were you thinking about?"

Abby leaned over and whispered, "You," before turning back to look at Jake. "Uh, sorry about that. What did you say?"

"We need to devise a new plan for this bastard. I didn't realize how fixated he is on you until we raided the cabin. I haven't heard from my men that he's been back, so he must have found another place to hole up."

They were starting from scratch again. The knowledge that he wanted her would only help in her cause. She hoped. They had missed the opportunity to catch him unaware, but that wasn't going to stop Abby. She just needed another big break, and she didn't know how she was going to pull that one off.

Sam pushed his chair back from the table. "Dinner was great, Emma, but I need to go to my house to make some calls, get another change of clothes, and check on a few things."

Abby rose. "I'll go with you."

"Oh no you don't, baby. You're safer here with them. You're the one he wants, remember?" He leaned down and placed a chaste kiss on her lips. Abby's brows knit together and she felt a frown forming on her face. Deflated she looked down.

John pushed his chair back, scratching it against the wood floors. "Don't worry, Mom. I'll go with him and make sure he doesn't skip town." Leave it to her kid to notice.

"I don't think that's a good idea, John. Why don't you stay here with me?" Abby's voice rose.

"Nah, I'll go with him. Just consider it some bonding time." John made quotes when he said bonding.

Abby walked them to the door. "Just to your house and back, right. No stopping for anything else." John had already disappeared outside the door and was climbing in the passenger side of the black SUV. Abby touched Sam's arm, stopping his exit. "You know this isn't going to be pleasant. You don't have to take him."

Sam pulled her into his arms and kissed the top of her head. "Yes, I do. We need to clear the air on some things." He cupped her chin and lifted it to his. His gaze held hers. "I'm not leaving, and he needs to know that. Besides, I'm sure he just wants to threaten me again." He leaned down and placed a soft kiss on her lips. Against her better judgment, she let them go as she stood on the porch and watched them drive away, taking her heart with them.

Kate Allenton

CHAPTER 17

Sam knew the silence in the car wouldn't last. He looked over at John and could tell he was busting at the seams to say something, so he took the edge off. Maybe if he told John, his son how he felt. He shook his head and smiled before whispering, "I have a son." His gaze traveled over to John again. "I love her, John, and there isn't anything you can say to make me leave her."

John's gaze turned from the apple trees they passed to Sam's eyes. "I haven't seen her happy in a long time, Sam. Don't get me wrong, she hasn't complained, and she's had a hard life raising me by herself."

Sam swallowed the lump in his throat, mourning all of those years lost with his son and with Abby. He wouldn't ever get them back. All he could do was move forward. "I won't hurt her or you." His voice cracked.

"I just want her to be happy; she deserves that."

"John, I promise I'll spend the rest of my life making her happy if she'll have me." Sam's gaze left the road to look at his son. "You know, she won't do anything that's going to make you miserable, so I guess you hold her happiness in your hands. I'm not stupid enough to think your opinion doesn't mean anything. But don't get me wrong, even if you don't agree, I won't ever give up on getting her back until the day I die."

"I guess that's a good thing. I'd hate to have to get my uncle to shoot you. You better make her happy, old man. I promise to try if you will."

Sam's pulse raced. Had his son just given him permission to date his mother? He knew if he could see own his face he would be grinning from ear to ear. This day had just gotten a whole lot better. Until his mind started thinking of everything that could go wrong. "We need to catch this guy."

Sam pulled up to his house and went inside with John on his heels. "How do you suppose we do that?"

"I wish I knew." Sam looked around his house to make sure nothing was out of place and was happy to find everything seemed as he'd left it. He grabbed some more clothes before checking his answering machine. The only message he had was one from Stone, saying he'd figured out the connection. Daley was here because of the woman he murdered. She had been a jury member. *Shit.* It couldn't be just coincidence that had brought that bastard to Abby's town. *Damn, if I wouldn't have come running because of the pentagram, he wouldn't have ever found out about her.* The last thing he wanted was for Abby or John to be put in harm's way, and if something happened to either one of him, he knew it would be his fault. Seeing Abby and finding out about John had changed his life. He hadn't needed to worry about anyone but himself since he'd stayed away from Abby, but now this changed everything.

"Can you stop by my house, too, so I can grab me and Mom some clothes? Emma's clothes look way too big on her."

"Sure," Sam said as he closed and locked the door behind them. "We need to make it quick. I'm sure your mom is going to be sending out a search party soon."

****

Richard Daley hadn't been expecting his nemesis and his offspring to find him, but he was prepared nonetheless. He had come to the little spitfire's house and had been waiting for her return. The syringes he held in his hand wouldn't have been for her, of course. No, he wanted her lucid for the plans he had. He had only hoped it would be Sam that brought her home. He had planned for Sam to watch, slowly destroying his spirit before he killed him and the petite brunette. He had finally figured out a name to add to the face. He could feel his pants tightening just thinking about Abby. He wanted her, and he'd have her, every way he pleased. It had taken them long enough. Richard had thought he might go crazy in this house, but the time he'd spent waiting proved interesting enough.

He's had time to snoop and get things ready for their little reunion. He gripped the two syringes in his hand as he peeked out the window and watched them walk toward the door. The kid was going to be the easiest. He moved to the kid's room and waited, tucked in the corner behind the closed door. Just a few more seconds and it would be one

Kate Allenton

down with one to go. He heard them rummaging through the house like a herd of cattle coming to a slaughter. He had been careful not to disturb much and alert them to his presence. No, this time, he was going to be careful.

He wouldn't ruin this like the slut had. Eighteen years ago, he'd picked her out of the jury box. She'd been young and pretty back then, easy to manipulate. A few promises of love and a life together and she was begging him not to leave her. It was because of her vote that he'd never gone down for that crime. The stupid bitch had never figured it out. She was another lose end he planned to tie up, along with the kid that had seen him leave the crime. They were the last ones left that held any cards over his freedom. He'd found her a month ago at the diner, and he'd had to grovel to get her back. He needed her to trust him again. He hadn't planned to kill her, but after the last threat she made about going to the police with the truth, he hadn't had any other choice. She had to die, just like Sam was about to.

He watched as the doorknob turned. The kid had his head turned, yelling back to Sam, who was probably in the living room. "Give me five minutes then we can go." As soon as he cleared the door, Richard waited to see if anyone was going to enter behind the kid, and when no one followed, he jammed the needle into the kid's neck and hit the plunger. It only took seconds for the kid to fall down. The look on his face was priceless. He couldn't wait to see Sam's face when it was his turn. Richard grabbed him before he hit the floor and dragged him the rest of the way into the room, closing the door behind him. He had stashed rope he would need to carry out his plans in all the rooms, even in the brat's.

Richard set the kid in a chair and grabbed the rope, tying it tight to make sure the kid didn't escape. He cursed. He hadn't been expecting the kid's weight, but it wasn't going to stop him. He wiped the sweat from his brow and cracked the door open. His nemesis would be in here soon enough to check on the kid. He pulled out John's cell and turned it off. He didn't want any interruptions as he carried out this plan.

He didn't have to wait long to hear Sam hollering for John to hurry up. He knew it would be just a matter of minutes before he came into the room and found John, succumbing to the same fate. Richard resumed his hiding spot behind the door and waited. The knob turned, and Sam walked in to his trap, just like his offspring had, unaware harm awaited them in their own home He plunged the needle into Sam's neck and caught his fall too. Sam's eyes widened, branding the look of horror into Richard's brain for the rest of his life.

The drug he'd procured from the black market paralyzed Sam. The doses he'd got were set to Sam's weight, not the kid's. He wanted Sam alive to watch what he had planned next. He didn't care if the kid saw or not. Sam's eyes moved back and forth, resting on John, and then trying to look at him from the corner of the eye. Richard whispered, "I can't wait until Abby gets here."

He could see the need to scream in Sam's eyes even though nothing came from his mouth. The drug wasn't going to last long. He'd need to make sure Abby came to him before the drug wore off. He only had two needles and hoped to kill Sam while he was still under the drug's influence. Richard dragged him down to the cellar and tied him into the awaiting chair, facing the small cot he had moved down there. Sam was going to have a front row seat. Richard smiled at the thought.

"Time to go get my girl," he said to Sam as he patted him on the head like a dog. "Don't have too much fun until we get back," he chided, and left him alone with his thoughts in the cellar.

Richard returned to the boy's room and took in his appearance. He knew he'd have to kill him, but he would have fun making Abby beg for his life. Richard walked around the unconscious boy, looking for something that was going to draw his mom's attention to the fact he was here and waiting. He decided on the intricate watch. He had seen pictures of her wearing the same one. "Yes, this will be enough to get her to come looking."

He unfastened the watch and left through the back of the house to give it to the one person he knew would call her. The little old lady had been jittery when he had tried to give her the rent money the same day cops converged on the lake cabin. His presence, along with the watch, all but assured him that the spitfire would be on her way.

He returned to the house after leaving the old lady. He had watched from the shadows as she picked up the phone and made her call minutes after his departure. Richard returned to the house to wait. He was going to use a different tactic with Abby. He had the kid's baseball bat in hand,

peering out the window as he waited
for her arrival.

CHAPTER 18

Abby kept herself busy, helping Emma clean the kitchen and stripping and replacing the sheets from their bed. Emma had produced a stash of Abby's clothes, which she'd left over months before. She'd changed into her comfortable jeans and had just pulled out a mop to start on the kitchen floor when she glanced at her watch. Two hours had passed, and she hadn't heard a word from them. Her fingers trembled as she went to her cell phone lying on the counter and punched in Sam's cell number. No answer. She left him an urgent message for him to call. She tried John's, too, but got the same thing. No answer. She dropped the mop and pushed through the kitchen door as Jake was walking toward her.

"I can't reach either of them. They've been gone two hours, and they won't answer their phones."

"Abby. I'm sure they're just bonding, but they have been gone a long time. We probably should find out where they are." Jake said with the same quotation marks around bonding that John had made earlier.

"Oh god, they've killed each other. That's why they aren't answering the phone." Deciding that she couldn't take anymore, Abby went to put her shoes on. "I'll kill them both, if they just got side tracked," she mumbled.

Jake stood in the hall, as she was coming back out of the bedroom door. "It's okay, Abby. We can track them with John's watch. Just come down into my office." An invisible weight lifted from her shoulders.

"Thank god you're such a nerd." Jake chuckled and threw his arm around her shoulder, leading her down the stairs. When she reached the door to his office, her cell phone rang. "Thank god," she whispered as she pulled it out and hit talk.

Abby's shoulders slumped. She thought she was going to scream. It wasn't her men on the other end. A sweet old voice chimed through the receiver. *Mrs. A.* "I'm sorry, Mrs. A. I can't talk right now. I'm in the middle of something."

Her next words were something a mother never wanted to hear. Mrs. A didn't know her words would spike up Abby's fear higher than she'd ever thought possible.

"That's okay, dear, you and Jake just wanted me to call when I saw Mr. Smith again, and he just left."

"Mrs. A, I'm going to put you on speaker. Jake is here with me, and I'd like for him to hear this."

"Sure, dear. Uh, hello? Hello, Jake, are you there, dear?"

"Hi, Mrs. A. It's nice to hear from you again." Abby filled him in on what Mrs. A said as Jake started pushing buttons on his monitor, trying to get a fix on John's watch.

"Uh, yes, dear. He just left my house. You remember me telling you that Mr. Smith had given me the locket, well when he showed up with this watch; I knew it had to belong to either one of your sisters or someone in your family. Would you be a dear and check to see if anyone lost theirs?"

Jake's monitor beeped and indicated John was at Mrs. A's house. Abby dropped the phone onto the counter as her hand went to cover her gaping mouth. "No..,please, dear god. No."

Jake picked up the phone. "Sorry about that, Mrs. A. It seems John is missing his watch. Did Mr. Smith by any chance tell you where he was going?"

"No, sorry, dear. He mentioned leaving town, but he seemed to be headed back in toward town."

Abby pulled herself from her morbid thoughts, and a spark of hope shot through her system. "Mrs. A, I'll be there in ten minutes. Do you mind holding on to his watch until I get there?"

Jake stared at Abby, his brows knit and his head tilted. He was probably wondering why the watch was so important to her when her son and lover were missing. She'd have to clue him in on the way. She grabbed the phone from the counter and Jake's arm, heading toward the door before Emma stopped them and brought reality crashing back down on her.

"Where ya'll headed in such a hurry?"

Abby walked toward Jake's SUV, with Emma by her side, she told her about John and Sam not answering their phones, and how John's watch had turned up at Mrs. A's.

"Wait," Emma screamed and ran back in the house only to walk out moments later with an ankle holster and gun. "You might need this."

"Emma, I don't know what I'd do without you." *Pull it together, Abby. They need you.* Her thought pulled her from her despair, and she refocused on getting her men back.

"You need to set up your guys to watch Emma. We're going to need Butch and Mike to help us." Abby climbed into Jake's SUV. She turned her attention back to Jake as he walked Emma back up to stand on the porch. They were in a tight embrace, and their kiss could have sizzled an egg like the pavement on a hot summer day. Abby didn't have to read lips to know what Emma said. She felt it in her heart for Sam. Abby pulled her cell and called Mike, who happened to be with Butch, and filled them in on what had happened and where they were going.

She was getting her men back, even if that meant killing the bastard, and she wasn't opposed to that This asshole needed to pay. *You don't screw with the people I love and get away with it.*

CHAPTER 19

Abby wasn't sure when she had turned from forensic investigator to playing the lead investigator into her own hell, but she found some comfort that the guys were with her and wouldn't let her down. Thank god, Mike had told the captain it was his plan, when he'd called it in. Abby couldn't believe both of them had been unable to overtake the older man and had been kidnapped. That thought alone scared her into stepping up her game. The moment she'd touched the watch, she had seen what he'd done to her son. He had stuck a needle in his neck, knocking him unconscious at her own damn house. At least that was in her favor. She smiled. She knew that house like the back of her hand. She knew every possible way to get in and the best way to advance on it to hide her movements. Mike had touched the object and got the same replay, telling the others about the state they were in. After seeing the way her son had fallen over, she knew something had paralyzed him. She hit her speed dial, calling in her trusty computer friend. Ted answered on the first ring.

"Hey, doll face. Do you need another favor?"

"You know me too well, Ted. I need you to run something through your computer but not just that. I need you to swing by the doc's office, pick up what I need, and meet me on Jenks, the street next to the woods. Can you do that for me?" Her hands trembled as she held the phone up to her mouth. She couldn't stop the fear rolling out of every pore of her body.

"Well, let's start with what you need in the computer. Your wish is my every command." She needed to remember all of the times he had helped her lately. She really needed to do something special for the guy. Maybe she'd sic Mrs. A on him and get him set up with a girl.

Abby paused. She'd do anything to keep one of her family member's safe, but it still didn't sit right with her to bring the computer geek into her danger. Heck, her family had taught her to take care of herself long before she joined the force. Even with all of that knowledge, her voice trembled as she spoke because she had no choice but to pull him into her chaos.

"I need to know what paralyzing agent is running around in the black market. I need the side effects, the length of duration, and then I need for you to do whatever you have to do, to get me the antidote."

"Hell yeah. This one is much better then running a stupid phone trace. Do you need any fire power too?" His excitement came through the line like a living thing, and Abby knew he meant well. It did nothing to settle her nerves.

"No, I think Mike and Jake have that covered. Besides, I have Emma's gun attached to my ankle. I'm not going in unarmed." She knew they'd do whatever she asked as long as it kept her safe. She really didn't want to wait on Mike. He would want to go in with guns blazing and shoot the bastard himself.

"Well, I think the name of the drug you're looking for is called suxamethonium chloride. It only lasts about an hour and is easily counteracted with atropine. That shouldn't be too hard to get my hands on. I'll meet you in fifteen minutes." He disconnected the call and all Abby could do was wait.

They waited at the destination, far enough from her house that he wouldn't notice and next to the woods so that she could enter from the side of her house near the water.

It would give her enough cover going in to get to the outside stairs leading to the basement. Richard Daley wasn't leaving that house alive, not after threatening John and Sam's lives. She still owed him for all of the lost years. Abby paced and twisted her hands as she waited on the reinforcements.

Jake walked to her and threw his arms around her. "Everything is going to be okay, Abby. We have the element of surprise on our side. He doesn't know about your ability of psychometry. He won't even think that you know what happened and if I had to bet, he's going to be expecting you to come through the front door." Jake pulled her close.

She relaxed in his brotherly hold, even though it did little to calm her nerves. His little pep talk did give her an idea. Abby pushed out of his arms. "You're right. He's going to be expecting me to come to the front door, and he isn't going to be expecting Butch or Mike. They could work as my diversion so I can get into the basement." She just about jumped up and down. "You're a genius."

Jake placed his hand on her shoulders. "You aren't going in alone, Abby. I'll send Butch and Mike to the front door, but we don't want to scare him into doing anything rash. We can't afford for him to hurt either one of them. Emma would never forgive me."

"Fine, Jake. He won't even hear us coming, but the bastard is mine. You only interfere when I say; otherwise, you stay out of sight. Abby pasted her hands on her hips while the terms of her conditions sank in.

"Abby, I'll interfere when I damn well please. I'm not going to let you get hurt. We don't know if he's armed or not. We already know the damage he can do. Look at the hostages he has. It ends today, here and now. Whether you take him out or I do. It's going to be over. Do you understand?" Jake crossed his arms over his chest and looked down on her as if she were a child. She'd take what she could get.

"Understood."

Reinforcements arrived, pulling up and parking next to them. Even Ted arrived at the same time. Abby ran to Ted as Jake discussed their plan with Butch and Mike. Abby stole a glance at her big brother. His face was red, and his arms were folded, plastered across his body. *He's not liking my plan.*

"You got what I need, wizard?" She slid up to him, rubbing her shoulder to his.

"Only if you're talking about my ability to get what you need, my lady." He bowed and handed her two capped syringes containing the clear liquid. She didn't want to inject Sam or John, but she would to save their lives.

"I need you to have EMS on standby. Have them roll in silent and wait until the dust clears. I'll feel better if they're nearby if the antidote doesn't work."

"When did you turn commando on me? It's such a turn-on." He bumped her shoulder again.

"While you were stuck behind your computer screen, sexy," she chided. "If it wasn't for you, I wouldn't be able to do my rescues. You're my Tonto." Abby leaned in and placed a quick kiss on his cheek before returning to the men who were now talking in hushed tones. She wasn't sure she was going to like what they were cooking up.

As she walked up, all conversation came to a halt. She noticed the quiet nods between the men. *Aww hell.*

Mike handed her a revolver that she tucked into the waistband in the back of her jeans. "We ready?"

Mike pulled her into his steel arms and kissed the top of her head. "Be careful." Butch took her out of Mike's arms and into his own embrace, kissing her on the cheek before whispering, "Kick his ass."

Abby smiled up at the men and turned to start her trek through the woods toward her house. Abby estimated the property that butted up to hers was about a half mile, but it felt like two. She heard the sounds of the grasshoppers and birds that had made their home in the overgrown grass and trees. She hoped that was all the wildlife that lived in there. Jake followed on her heels.

Her house came into view, and she dropped into the overgrown grass, thankful it was high and thick enough to hide their presence. She saw Mike's SUV pull up next to her driveway. The damn orange cones were still there. Butch wasn't anywhere in sight.

Abby whispered to Jake, "Where the hell is Butch?"

When Jake didn't reply, she crouched down and made her way to the side of the house. Mike was making a ruckus up front, banging on her door. She knew that at least his presence had been made known. She hoped theirs wasn't.

Abby peeked into the tiny basement window, and her heart dropped to her stomach. Rope held Sam secured to a chair in the middle of a room, and a cot had been placed in the corner. She made her way down the stairs to the basement. She pulled the key from the hiding place and quickly made headway of unlocking the door, opening only one of the two doors. The squeak alone from the left door was enough to wake the dead. Jake gave her a sign that the coast was still clear and returned to her side. They entered the big basement on silent feet, catching the door behind them and gently pulling it closed. Abby uncapped the syringe. She leaned next to his ear, hoping that he understood what she was about to do. "I'm sorry."

She plunged the antidote into his neck and pushed the plunger. She made quick work of the ropes that held him to the chair. The antidote seemed to be working. His eyes went wide, and he shook his head no. Abby whispered to Jake, "You need to get him somewhere safe then come back. I'll wait for you so we can find John."

Sam shook his head fiercely. It was evident he didn't want to leave.

Jake whispered, "I'm not fucking leaving you here."

Abby pulled the gun from her waist and had it pointing toward the floor. "I'll never forgive you if anything happens to him. Get him out of here. I'd take him myself, but I can't lift his weight." Abby didn't wait for a reply, although she thought she heard him cuss as she opened the door in the basement that leads into the house and slipped out of sight.

****

"God damn it." Jake searched the room frantically for an answer to his prayers. He came across a closet in the corner. He picked Sam up and set him inside before whispering, "It's okay. I'm not going to let anything happen to her."

Before he could shut the door, he heard the door to the basement open again. He stepped into the closet and gently pulled the door closed, in case it wasn't Abby, and he'd have been half-right. Daley walked into the basement with his arm around her neck. Jake pulled his phone and sent a text to Butch, telling him to get ready and to let Mike know. Jake didn't have to wait long watching through the slit in the door. He heard the door break upstairs, and Butch entered through the basement door with his gun drawn and sights set on Richard.

Richard glanced to the ropes that lay strewn across the floor and the empty chair and increased his hold on her neck. "It seems you've rescued the audience I had planned. No matter, this asshole can watch instead." Richard pulled a gun from somewhere and held it to her head. "Drop it or she dies."

Butch's eyes plead with hers, to shoot the bastard, but she shook her head no. She choked out, "Butch, this bastard's mine."

"Such big talk for a little girl. I'll have you begging me to kill you before I'm finished with you."

"Now who's talking shit, asshole?" Abby choked out.

"I can feel that thing sticking in my back, and trust me when I tell you, you need to look into a thing called penis enhancement."

Richard flexed his muscles, cutting off her air supply. "Drop it."

Butch leaned over and placed his weapon on the floor, and Richard's hold relaxed around her throat. She coughed. "I'll tell you what, Richard. You and me. If you win, I come willingly and he won't interfere. If I win, you let my son go."

He leaned into her and ran his tongue up her cheek. Abby tried to turn her face from his assault, but he wasn't giving her an inch. "This is going to be fun. Don't worry, love. Since Sam isn't here, I'll videotape it for him and send it in the mail. Tell the Neanderthal not to move. If he does, you'll never know what I did with your kid."

Abby clenched her jaw. Since Mike hadn't come to the basement, she hoped he'd found John unharmed. "Butch, move back toward the door and don't interfere."

Butch didn't answer her plea. He just moved out of the way. Richard loosened his hold enough for Abby to take advantage of it. She hit his groin, used her weight to fall down to the floor, and swept his legs out from underneath him. Richard Daley suddenly lay on the floor, staring up at the ceiling. Her victory was short lived when he swung his leg around, dropping her to the floor. Abby rolled out of his reach and sprang to her feet. "You just taught me a valuable lesson, Daley."

"What was that, love?" Richard was on his hands and knees, trying to catch his breath to push himself up.

Abby lifted her leg up and kicked him in the face. "Never underestimate your opponent, asshole."

Abby kicked him in the ribs. When he turned his face to look up at her, she punched his face, making sure the bastard was staying down.

She heard the bones in his nose crack as blood squirted across her concrete floor. "Richard Daley, you're under arrest. You have the right to remain silent." Abby walked over and picked up Butch's gun, handing it to him as Jake jumped from the closet, scaring the crap out of her. She continued. "Anything you say can, and will, be used against you in a court of law." Abby hunkered down near the closet door, in front of Sam half-sitting, propped up against the back of the closet wall. His functions seemed to be slowly returning.

Butch screamed, "Abby, watch out!" She turned toward Richard. He had a gun pointed in her direction and squeezed the trigger. Reacting on instinct, Abby threw her arms wide to protect Sam and felt the impact of the bullet in her chest. The power of the hit flung her forward into Sam's lap. Blood oozed inside her shirt. She put her fingers in the wet, sticky stuff and brought them up to her failing eyes. "Crap."

Gunfire erupted in her basement, coming from Butch and Jake's directions. Abby pulled the gun from her ankle holster and pointed it in Richard's direction, but she was too late. He lay unresponsive, dead on her floor. Abby dropped the gun and relaxed into Sam's arms, turning to kiss the muscled arm holding her.

"Go find our son," she squeaked to Jake and Butch. Her eyes were heavy. Unable to keep them open, she wasn't sure if they had carried out her orders. She closed her eyes and let the darkness claim her.

CHAPTER 20

Abby lay motionless, unable to move. *Squeak.* She knew where she was. She knew that damn door. *Squeak.* Abby lifted her eyelids to find the most beautiful vision in the world. Sam and John stood on each side of her. She could feel the press of their hands and hear their whispered words. "I told you to keep her safe," John said to his father.

"You were there, Junior. He got the drop on you, too, but you should have seen your mom kick his ass. She was like an angel sent down from heaven to save my sorry butt." Sam's eyes gleamed with pride.

A tear fell from her eye as she watched her men discussing her, not realizing she was awake.

John visibly swallowed the lump in his throat. "Dad, is she going to be okay?"

Abby couldn't take anymore. Had her son just called Sam dad? More tears fell from her eyes. She hadn't thought she would ever hear those words come from his mouth. Well, it could have turned out been better. She was lying in a hospital bed after all. Abby shook as her sobs grew.

"Oh god, Abby, are you hurting?"

"Mom, tell me where it hurts, and I'll get the doctor."

"I'm not crying because I'm hurt, John. I'm crying because my dream just came true. You two are with me and aren't tying to kill each other." Abby lifted her arm and wiped at the tears falling uncontrollably down her face.

John pushed Sam out of the way when he had leaned over to kiss the top of her head. "She's my mom. Get out of the way." John placed his kiss on her cheek.

Sam pushed John back. "Well, she's going to be my wife." He planted a gentle kiss on her lips.

Abby pushed him up, her gaze searching his face. "What did you say?"

Sam looked at John. "I told you she was going to be all right." John chuckled as Sam brought his gaze back down to her. "Abby Bennett, I've loved you all my life and can't imagine my world without you in it. Will you marry me?"

The waterworks started again. She was powerless against all of the feelings running through her heart. For once in her life, she thought she just might get her happy ending.

"Mom, put the old man out of his misery and answer him already." John stood with his arms crossed over his chest.

"Ryan Douglas, Sam Bennett, whatever the hell your real name is, of course I'll marry you."

Tension seemed to vanish from his shoulders as he leaned down and planted a tender kiss on her lips. "I'll love you forever."

Leave it to her son to break the mood. "It's about damn time."

EPILOGUE

Abby stood staring in the mirror when Emma and Claire walked into the room. She heard their gasps and didn't need to turn around to see what had caught their attention. She felt beautiful. Her white satin dress hugged her body. She felt like a princess as she gazed at her reflection in the mirror.

Emma waddled to her, placing her arms around her. Her baby bump made the hug awkward. "You look beautiful."

"Stop or you'll make me cry."

Claire walked to her other side, and Abby saw her sister's reflection smile in the mirror. "He's a lucky man."

A tear fell down her cheek. They left the room to find Mike waiting for her in the living room of the beach house. He held out his arm to her, and she placed hers through it. "You're beautiful inside and out, baby sister. Mom and Dad would be so proud of the woman you've become."

Mike walked her out the back patio door, stopping on the top of the stairs. Chairs filled with the people she cared about sat in a row, but her gaze passed them to the two men standing at the altar. Abby was speechless, they took her breath away. John stood there, dashing in a tuxedo, at his father's side as the best man.

She carefully maneuvered the steps and looked up at Sam again. He held her gaze as she travelled the short walkway up to his side. She hadn't worn a veil. Mike held her hand out to Sam, and Sam pulled her close, whispering in her ear, "Abby you're beautiful, baby."

His black tuxedo stretched across his chest, hid his muscles from her view. There was no denying her attraction to this man. The man she would be spending the rest of her life with. The man she'd spent her adult life trying to find. Another tear fell down her cheek. Her heart was full for the first time in eighteen years. "I love you."

The ceremony was enough that she would remember it the rest of her life. Her surprise came when the minister spoke. "Ryan Mitchell Douglas a.k.a., Sam Bennett, do you take Abigail Marie Bennett to be your wife?"

Everyone in attendance started laughing.

After the "I do's Sam picked her up and carried her to the beach house next door.

"Why are we going over here?" she asked as she laid her head on his chest. She knew he would take care of her for the rest of his life.

"The first property I bought when I could afford it. I knew I couldn't come here and chance running into you again, but a guy can dream." Sam walked through the open door, with her still in his arms.

"Back to where it all began for us." Her heart was again whole. Abby kissed his cheek.

"I think John needs a little brother, don't you?" Sam said as he kicked the door closed with his foot.

Abby realized her future was just beginning.

The End

If you enjoyed my story, please leave a comment on Amazon.

If you would like to sign up for my newsletters about upcoming releases, please go to www.kateallenton.com.

Enjoy an excerpt from the book 3 in the Bennett Sister's Saga,

Mind Play:

Butch and Claire's Book

Tentative Release July 2012

Claire Bennett stood with a champagne flute in hand watching her family and friends as they mingled during her latest fundraiser. "Two down and one to go," she whispered to herself as she spotted her older brother, Mike across the room. Her two sisters had gotten married over the last year, and her middle sister, Emma, was nine months pregnant. Now, if Claire had anything to say about it, it was Mike's turn to settle down.

Mrs. Anderson, the town gossip, glided up to her side and followed Claire's gaze. "I see the wheel's turning, Claire. What do you have in mind for your brother?"

Claire glanced to the old woman standing beside her and her lips tilted up in a smile. Everyone always wondered where Mrs. A. got her gossip; no one would have guessed the two of them were in cahoots together where her family was concerned. Mrs. A had trusted Claire, telling her of a promise Mrs. A had once made to Claire's mother on her deathbed. She was an outsider watching over her and her siblings as they grew up. Like a guardian angel, she had always been there for each of them without the truth being known. Claire had been the only one to catch on to the old lady's tactics. She'd paid attention and noticed when Mrs.

A played a part in not only keeping their secrets, but also in keeping them out of trouble.

"I think it's Mike's turn to be happy and settle down, and the way he's staring at Dr. Elizabeth Lister, I think we've found his match, Don't you?"

Mrs. A rubbed her hands together and smiled with a gleam in her eyes. "Good choice, Claire. I think the little doctor would be perfect, but you're brother sure is stubborn."

"I agree, just look at him. He hasn't been able to take his eyes off of Elizabeth, since she walked into the room." Claire had grown accustomed to seeing the scowl on Mike's face, her entire life. There weren't many people that would have seen the sparkle in his eyes that accompanied said scowl. She'd noticed it more and more, when he'd been around the little doctor. Their chemistry was a living thing when put in a room together. They were just both going to need a nudge in the right direction.

"I think it's time to work our magic." Mrs. A said as she glided away in the direction of her brother. It was all coming together. She'd thought long and hard about the plans she had for her family. How they could find happiness, even with their "gifts." Truth be told, Emma and Abby hadn't needed her help, they had found their own happily ever after. She hadn't needed to interfere, but she would for her brother. Mike was a detective for the Southall PD, and worse, he was as stubborn as a mule. He didn't socialize much, and she'd never seen him date anyone serious or otherwise, but that was all about to change.

Fingers touched Claire's waist, tugging her back against a broad muscular chest. The manly scent of cologne hit her nose. She was about to turn around swinging, when Butch whispered in her ear. "When are we going to run away together, Angel? Can't you just see it, you lounging around a beach in your bikini with me by your side. Cocktails in our hands enjoying the beautiful sunset in Maui as the waves crash against the seashore."

Claire closed her eyes and let his description take hold. She could clearly see what he was offering, if only he had meant it. She opened up her eyes again and pulled out of his embrace. "I think you've got the wrong girl. Maybe you should have made a play for Abby."

"Aw Angel, don't be like that. Abby and I are just friends; you're the sister that's going to rock my world." Butch winked at her.

Claire threw he head back and laughed. "Now I know you're screwing with me. I've never rocked anyone's world. And I'm afraid a girl like me, couldn't keep up with a guy like you."

Before Butch could reply, Claire's younger sister, Emma, and brother-in-law, Jake walked up. "Great party, Claire, but I think I'm going to have to take Emma home and put her to bed." Jake said, putting a protective arm around Emma's expanded waist.

Her obstetrician had told them, it was only a matter of days, before she delivered.

Worry made Claire's heart speed up. "Are you alright, do I need to go grab Dr. Lister? I'm sure she wouldn't mind taking a look at you since she's here."

"Don't be ridiculous." Emma turned her attention to the doctor in question. "She's having a good time. I'm sure I just need to rest." Emma said returning her gaze to Claire, giving her a small smile.

Claire wasn't sure she believed her sister, but didn't have a chance to reply.

"Excuse me, Ms. Bennett." Claire turned to find her assistant standing next to her.

"Emma, Jake, Butch this is Jenny, my new assistant. She's the one that is going to keep me organized with all of my new fundraisers."

Butch took a hold of Jenny's hands and raised it to his lips giving her knuckles a gentle kiss. "It's a pleasure to meet you Jenny."

Jenny's cheeks reddened from Butch's greeting. She'd get use to Butch's flirting ways. They all had at some point.

Jenny looked down at the ground and replied. "You too." She raised her gaze again to meet Claire's. "Claire, I just wanted to tell you that I've taken care of the caterer and the band, and I have a few receipts I'm going to put in your office. I have a few more things to take care of, but I wanted to remind you the cleaning crew would be coming by at ten in the morning."

"Oh my god." Emma said as she leaned forward, with one hand clutching Jake's arm and the other around her swollen belly.

"What, what's the matter?" Jake asked in a panic.

Blood was draining from Emma's face, turning it a ghostly shade of white. "No one panic, but I think my water just broke."

Claire glanced at her assistant. "Find Mike and Abby, tell them Emma's water broke and we're going to the hospital. You're in charge." Claire said as she took Emma's arm and helped her out of the front door. She took a chance and looked up at Jake and Butch. Both of them looked as if they were going to faint. It would have been comical, had she not needed them to focus on Emma.

"Jake, where are you parked?" Claire asked, when she didn't get a reply, she snapped her fingers. "Focus Jake, where are you parked?"

"I...I don't know."

"It's ok Jake, we'll take the limo. My driver is outside, and he'll get us there in no time. Help me get Emma settled in, and I'll take care of everything." Claire made a beeline to her limo and helped lower Emma gently inside, before climbing in after her. Jake and Butch each took a seat. Claire tapped on the partition and waited for it to slide down.

"Where to Ms. Bennett?" Stan, her limo driver, asked.

"Get us to the hospital, fast. Emma's in labor." Before the window had risen back in place, Stan was pulling out of her drive and hitting the gas. Claire moved to sit next to Emma. "How far apart are the contractions?"

Emma screamed and doubled over panting.

Claire took her hand and gently squeezed it, "Emma, look at me."

Emma turned her head and looked up at her sister.

"Just breathe Emma, remember what they taught you, in through your nose and out through your mouth. Breathe through the contractions." Sweat had started to bead on Emma's forehand, but she nodded that she'd heard.

Claire pulled her phone she had stashed inside her bra and hit speed dial. The fact that Butch hadn't commented on the move, told her enough to know he wasn't going to be any help. She'd set the hospital and the obstetrician's numbers in her phone, just in case. She'd told the hospital and her doctor, they were on their way and guessed at how far apart the contractions were. They were now expecting them, and once they got there Claire would relax. She hadn't expected Butch and Jake to lose brain cells and not be able to function, but Claire had been prepared, and it was a good thing too.

Claire felt the temperature change in the limo, turning the air cooler before Emma said a word. "Not now old woman" Emma spat out through gritted teeth. Jake had pulled himself from his stupor and was now rubbing Emma's back as she was slumped over, whispering words of encouragement and love in her ear.

The limo pulled up to the hospital in record time. The staff was waiting outside with a wheelchair to push Emma in with Jake on her heels. Claire and Butch made their way to the small waiting room, making themselves as comfortable as could in the hard chairs. Claire rose and walked to the vending machine for a cup of coffee, when she had felt Butch behind her again, before he whispered in her ear. "Doesn't that beach sound good, Angel?" Butch placed his hands again on her hips and placed a light kiss on her neck.

Claire maneuvered out of his embrace and swatted at his arm. "Butch, knock it off."

Mike and Abby showed up. Mike started his pacing as he bantered back and forth with Butch, about what state of mind Jake might be in. Abby took a seat next to Claire and put her arm around her shoulders. "You did good, sis. She's going to be all right, and just think, in a few short hours, we are going to have a niece or nephew to spoil."

A few short hours turned into several long hours until Jake emerged, walking in dressed in scrubs. The talking and the pacing stopped as they all stood there waiting for news of Emma and the baby. The color had returned to his face and he graced them with a huge smile. "Emma did great, and Lily is as beautiful as her mother."

Claire let out a breath, and pulled Abby into a hug, as Butch and Mike congratulated Jake and shook his hand. "When can we see her?" Claire asked.

"They're moving her from the birthing room into a regular room in a few minutes. I'll come back and get you when they have her settled."

Claire and Butch settled in the limo for the ride back to her house, after seeing Emma and Lily. She kicked off her stilettos and sunk into the leather of the cushioned seats of the limo. She'd be glad out of her dress and climb into her bed. Jake had been right, she was beautiful. Lily had a head full of brown hair like her mother's, and slept while Claire had held her. Night had turned into day while they had been with Emma in the hospital and Claire was exhausted. Her bed had been calling her name for the last several hours. Butch slid closer and put his arm around Claire's shoulder settling her into the crook of his arm. "You did good, Angel. Now just close your eyes and I'll wake you when we get there."

Claire leaned into the warmth he offered and did just what he asked.

She closed her eyes and let sleep
take hold of her. She'd dreamed of
the beach Butch teased her about,
the picture he had painted about the
both of them. Those hours dreaming
of a vacation she'd never have were
some of the best sleep she'd had in a
long time. There weren't any death
threats hanging over her family, like
previous months. Her sleep was
peaceful.

Claire woke up to find herself in
her room with a smile on her face.
How had she got there? She didn't
remember anything after falling
asleep nestled in Butch's arms in the
limo. Movement in her bed had her
head jerking to the left. Butch lay on
top of the covers next to her. Claire's
mouth dropped open, and her hand
flew to cover it as she stared at him.

Butch blinked open his eyes
slowly and smiled. He said, "Good
morning, Angel," while his hand
reached out and pulled her body
close to his. The thin barrier of her
dress, the sheets, and the comforter
were the only thing standing in the

way of their bodies becoming intimate.

Claire put her palms on his chest and pushed. "Butch, why are you in my bed?"

Butch rubbed his eyes. "Because I carried you upstairs and your bed looked so comfortable."

Claire pushed out of his arms, slid from under the covers throwing her legs over the edge of the bed and stood. "There are five other rooms on this floor with beds just like mine, why didn't you pick one of those?"

"Don't get uptight, Angel, I didn't touch you. I didn't undress you. I didn't let my hands roam all over your sweet tight body. I didn't kiss your soft red lips. I was a good boy, but we can change all of that right now if you want to climb back in bed."

I hope you enjoyed it.

Please visit my website at
www.KateAllenton.com

For updates on the release.

ABOUT THE AUTHOR

Kate has lived in Florida for most of her entire life. She enjoys a quiet life with her husband and two kids.

Kate has pulled all-nighters finishing her favorite books and also writing them. She says she'll sleep when she's dead or when her muse stops singing off key.

She loves creating worlds full of suspense, secrets, hunky men, kick ass heroines, steamy sex and oh yeah the love of a lifetime. Not to mention an occasional ghost and other supernatural talents thrown into the mix.

Made in the USA
Columbia, SC
10 November 2017